To mom and dad.
To my brothers and sisters.
To the communities that raised me.
Thank you for helping to make my life interesting and meaningful.
Thank you for teaching me about the importance
of loving one another.

CONTENTS

PREAMBLE

by Carson Dodge

July 18, 1967

Mrs. Snowden said that a preamble is a preparatory statement or an introduction—like the preamble to the constitution. I asked her, "Does that mean it is written first? Did the fathers of our country write the preamble to the constitution and then they wrote the constitution?"

She thought about it for a moment, and I saw her face scrunch up, and then said, "No. They probably did not write the preamble first. It would seem more likely they wrote it last."

"So you can write a preamble last, even though it becomes first?"

"Yes," she said.

"Could someone write a preamble in the middle?" I asked.

"I'm not quite sure what you mean."

"Do you think it's possible they might have written the preamble after they had started the constitution, but before they were done?"

"That does seem possible, though I had never before considered that possibility, Carson. Why do you ask?"

"Oh, for no reason, I suppose. I guess I was just thinking of pre-ambles today." And with that I told yet another lie to my favorite teacher.

I have told so many lies to people I care about in the past eight and a half months, some whom I love, and I hate it. I even hate myself at times, for somehow, accidentally becoming a liar. How in heaven's name did I end up on this path? I honestly cannot remember lying intentionally to mom or dad in the first 11 years of my life. I was taught it wasn't right. Jesus said the truth shall set you free. And I believed that and still want to. So how did things end up this way? How did I get here?

How is it possible that someone could have a near perfect life for so many years, only to have it ripped away in an instant? I was so close to them and then they were gone. I had no idea I would lose them. Not even the thought that I "could" lose them. And then to have no one in my world understand at all what had happened. Why couldn't dad understand, or mom? I really thought given time that she would understand, but instead over time it became more than clear that this was an impossibility. I thought I was going crazy for a while. I couldn't sleep. I became a weird shadow of myself. A situation like this is really tough on a person when he is only eleven.

Have you ever had something happen in your life that simply changed everything? Something that, once it happened, you could never think of anything else, even great things, without also at the same time being reminded about the really bad thing that had occurred. Maybe that is how Jackie Kennedy felt that day in Dallas four years ago, when shots rang out around her. It ended up that she was safe, but her husband was not, and everything in her life going forward was forever changed. Completely different.

My situation is not tragic like hers, but it is perplexing for sure. I can't explain it to anyone. It may be that Phil understands somewhat, but he sees the world so differently from me. He has always been good to me, but that doesn't mean we are close. It's hard to explain. He marches to the beat of a different drummer for sure, and I think it's hard to be close to someone like that. I mean, what is he? And..., how does he seem to know about things in the future?

Another sleepless night. I guess I should be getting used to them by now. We had a really powerful thunderstorm—the third one this past week. Such things happen pretty often in south central Kansas, and it can be hard to sleep after those. I guess I'll do what I often do when I cannot sleep. I'll start re-reading the letters and stories I have sent to those in my life who have disappeared. The letters that likely no one is reading. It's a tough thing to try to communicate with those who are living in a world that is fifty years in the future. But trying to reach out to them has been my only way of trying to stay sane. Maybe I'll make yet another attempt to begin sending the letters again.

WHAT HAPPENED TO MY WORLD?

Letter One

January 16, 1967

Dear Larry and Harry,

This is your younger, brother, Carson Dodge. I am writing to you from out of the past, I think. It is January 16, 1967. I live at 777 So. Beck Street, in Wichita, Kansas. You guys are my twin brothers, six years older. I recently turned 11 and in the next few weeks you will be 17, and I have a big problem.........The day after Thanksgiving, 1966, you two disappeared. I mean, I woke up in the morning in the basement that serves as our bedroom, your beds had not been slept in, and you simply were not there.

I went looking for you and you were nowhere to be found. Then I asked mom, and she said, "Larry and Harry who?" You think I wasn't freaking out at that point? I asked dad, and he just gave me a strange look, like maybe I was bothering him. Our older sister, Sara, was home for Thanksgiving from college. I asked her and she thought I was joking and started tickling me. Some help she was. I was genuinely befuddled.

And then it started getting *really* weird. I looked at the family picture above the china cabinet in the dining room and guess what...you guys were not in it. Instead of being a family of nine, we had become a family of seven. Isn't this crazy? No one remembers who you two are nor who you were. No one except me. The closest I came to getting anyone to consider my point of view was with mom. I asked her..." Why would there be three beds in the basement where I sleep if I am the only one who sleeps there?" Mom paused and seemed at a loss for words.

Am I going crazy? I honestly don't think so. Here is my best explanation. Two weeks ago I was with two of my buddies watching a really neat, new TV show, called Star Trek, at one of their houses. In the episode we were watching something like my situation happened to my favorite character, whose name is Spock. Perhaps you have seen the show. Spock was caught in what they referred to as a time warp which put him into a parallel universe. Anyway, I think perhaps that is what has happened here. Now I am asking myself--Can I get you back? And, will I ever see you again? Because I am really pretty sure I have not gone crazy.

I still go to church like we do in our family.... Sunday school at 9:00 am., morning services at 10:30. Evening service at 6:00 pm., and Wednesday evening service at 7:00 pm each and every Wednesday. I have to admit that sometimes on Sunday evening I wish I could stay home and watch Wonderful World of Disney, but that is not allowed because we are a family that goes to evening services.

I was used to having you guys around and it started getting kind of lonely, so a few weeks ago I began sitting on the back row at church with Phil Ruger. You guys are probably asking, "What are you doing on the back row? That doesn't seem right." But you guys always liked Phil, he has always been nice to me, and sometimes when the sermons get boring he tells me interesting stories.

Last Sunday night it was just Phil and me. That is when Phil gave me something that caused me to conclude that you two may be caught in a time warp or a parallel universe. He gave me this small rectangular plastic thing that looked like the tiniest TV I have ever seen. He called it a "cell foam." I have no idea why he called it that. It has a very small screen but with a great, detailed picture, and get this—it is in color. I could not believe that. The only time I had ever seen a color TV was in Arkansas City at our cousins' house on the Fourth of July. The sound on this cell foam wasn't always great but I could make out most of what people were saying and the picture was always fantastic. I discovered in time that the cell foam had lots of short movies on it. They are similar to 8-millimeter movies (like the Zabruder movie from Dallas when JFK was shot) except that they have sound, and the pictures are way better. Phil said I could keep it for a week and today is Thursday. I have watched many of the movies on this thing, and some of them twice.

The movies on this device are what have convinced me that you two are still very much alive and are in some other time. I am pretty sure I saw both of you on several occasions. You look older and not as skinny and your hair is no longer auburn—it is gray, but I feel certain it is you. As twins you still look remarkably alike. I noticed that on this device there is a button that says Messenger. When I pressed the Messenger button, I found that it provided a way for me to type. That is why I am typing this letter to you and when I am done, I will press the send button and hope for the best. By the way, one of your buddies, Jay Bowser, has been giving me Dutch Rubs regularly on my way home from school. I know at heart he is a good guy, but if you get back to my time soon, would one of you please slug him.

Some of the movies on this cell foam may have been in 2015 but most were in 2016, which puts you 50 years ahead of me. Please tell me that the Kansas University Jayhawks have won at least one National Football Championship by 2017. I get so tired of listening to Oklahoma and Nebraska fans bragging.

By the way... I need to warn you about something I saw in one of the movies of you two at a party or a gathering. A person you were speaking with acted like a friend, but when his jacket opened slightly, I saw he was carrying a gun! And as I watched the movie longer, I saw the jacket of another person open who was also acting like a friend and he, too, had a gun. And neither of these guys were policemen. Who does that? Not dad, nor any of his friends. Not Uncle Bob or Uncle Wallace. Please be careful.

Many of the movies on the cell foam told me about things going on in 2016, though they would at times reference things in history, most of which are of course still in the future for me. I guess we really will get to the Moon, which is cool, and we will get there before the Russians, which I think is neat. I think someone said the Mets won a World Series—Wow! Lots of interesting things. But, most of the movies focused on the 2016 U.S. Presidential election and I have some questions for you. I think one of the candidates was a lady, which really surprised me. I had not considered the possibility that a woman could be President. I am still thinking about that. The other candidate was the Republican, like us. I think his name was Mr. Trump, but I'm not sure. In case I have his name wrong, I would simply say that he has an extraordinary head of hair and honestly, I would call him a super-bully of some sort. I think you will know who I am talking about.

So, Mr. Trump came across as this mean guy in the movies I watched. I honestly have never, ever seen or even heard of bullying like he displayed. He would have definitely been expelled by the principal at McCormick Elementary school for his bullying behaviors. He was quite mean with the way he treated the other Republican candidates. He did a lot of name calling—Low Energy Jeb, Lyin' Ted, Little Marco, on and on. The Little Marco name made me mad because the guys in our family tend not to be tall. I think dad would take him to task if he made fun of dad being short—it's not smart to mess with WWII vets. But I suppose Mr. Trump is probably a distinguished Veteran himself.

One day there was a movie of Mr. Trump getting off of a bus, and the sound was good on this movie. He bragged about treating women in ways that I am positive are not right. He talked about grabbing them and doing things to them they probably don't want to do. What he said seemed incredible...

Sometimes he would speak to large crowds of people and he seemed to say things that made the people like him, and at the same time be angry, and at the same time feel hate toward other people. He said mean things about Mexicans and especially about Muslims. Why would he say mean things about Muslims? Don't they simply understand who God is a little differently from us? Does that make them bad or wrong?

The thing that most astounded me is he made fun of a disabled reporter. If you haven't watched some of these movies, I am not joking. He really did make fun of a disabled reporter. I promise. If I did that, and dad found out about it, I would not be able to sit down or walk for a week, and I would absolutely deserve it. The board of education would be applied to the seat of knowledge, if you know what I mean.

I was obviously surprised when Mr. Trump won the presidency, but the next short movie surprised me more. The reporter could have been lying but he said that 80% of Evangelicals voted for Mr. Trump. I was thinking that **we** are Evangelicals, but I wasn't sure. Earlier this afternoon I called the church office and spoke with Sister Warner, and she said we are indeed Evangelicals, so I guess I have my answer.

I do not know for sure how you two voted, but I would bet my best two silver dollars that you were both in the 20% of Evangelicals who voted differently. Nevertheless, I think it is likely the reporter was telling the truth about Evangelicals in your time. I saw a movie of a group of people in a church like ours who were discussing the presidential election and only one person was speaking out and saying that she didn't think electing Trump was a good idea. Another lady said somewhat sternly to her, "At least we will be done with Ro B. Wade, and maybe gay marriage too." I have no explanation for that mysterious statement. I have a buddy at school named Bo so I assume Ro is a guy. Maybe Ro is a bad guy. I don't know what gay marriage is--maybe happy? Why in the world would we want to get rid of happy marriages? That lady's statement made no sense to me.

If you two get this message, and one of you lives near Wichita, there is a loose board on the front porch railing behind the porch swing. If you can answer some of my questions, please write the answers down in ink, not pencil which could fade, and put the paper under the loose board. You might want to wrap it in plastic. I know this might not work but I would like to hear from you. I will check under the board often. The questions I have for you have to do with how things will change or may change in the next 50 years, especially connected to things that are taught in church.

In Sunday School at Southwest Prairie Church I have been taught that we should all live our lives according to the example set by Jesus and how he lived—compassion and concern for all—all persons are our brothers and sisters (even Mexicans and Muslims). We are, as much as possible, to love one another. We are to be good stewards and take care of the earth for people in the future. We are to be honest, and even be cautious about white lies. We are never, ever, ever to be bullies. I mean to tell you, every one of my Sunday School teachers has taught these things to me and Reverend Warner says the same things in his sermons *when I listen,* which often I do.

So, here are the questions:

1. In the next 50 years will the K. U. Jayhawks win at least one football Championship? Please say yes.
2. Do people enjoy living on the moon, or is it kind of bor-

ing?

3. Did they ever figure out exactly who shot JFK, were others involved, and why?

4. Does LBJ get another 4 years or will we maybe get to try Barry Goldwater like mom and dad would like to do?

5. I've been hearing things about this black Christian minister, Martin Luther King. Does he end up becoming a helpful leader? Maybe a senator or something? He seems interested in making things better for black people which to me seems important.

6. Finally, why would Christians like us support a super-bully who lies a lot? This doesn't make sense to me.

I am hoping this whole parallel universe thing gets fixed soon. My world was much better with you guys in it. And, thank you for trying to help.

Your brother,

Carson

I MUST TELL YOU SOME BAD NEWS

Letter Two

March 25, 1967

Dear Larry and Harry,

T his is your 11-year-old brother writing to you again from 1967. If you get this letter but did not see the first one, I sent it on January 16. In the first letter I explained that as hard as it must be for you to believe, it appears you, or possibly I have been caught in a "time warp" which leaves us in parallel universes for the time being. I have no idea whether an older version of me is in your other universe, 50 years ahead of this one, but the two of you are definitely not here. You both disappeared the day after Thanksgiving, 1966, and I am the only person in this universe who remembers you. It has not been pleasant.

Let me start by saying I got a few things wrong. I called this device that Phil came up with a "cell foam" and he later pointed out that it is called a "cell phone." He has watched some of the movies I have watched, and he was able to determine that this small device with the short movies on it is a type of phone. I never considered that. It did not have a cord, and no rotary dial. I honestly thought it was some sort of futuristic TV. Fortunately, Phil found a way to recharge the battery. He lets me use this phone a few days each week. I watch the movies on it again and again. He told me there are a few additional movies on the phone—of girls in swimsuits, but that at my age I probably shouldn't watch them, so I haven't.

I must tell you some bad news. I have done some really rotten things since I sent my first letter to you two months ago. I just have not been myself since you guys disappeared from my life. At church I've heard it said that confession is good for the soul, so here goes...

The first is that I did something awful to your buddy, Jay Bowser. You both know that Jay Bowser is this tall, lanky guy, but he is not tall and skinny. He is tall and big, and certainly much bigger than me. He was giving me Dutch Rubs regularly when he would see me on the way home from school, and I didn't like it. He may have assumed they didn't bother me because he was thinking I liked him which is actually true. I like Jay Bowser and always have. But he is much bigger than me and I got really tired of getting Dutch Rubs, and apparently, he wasn't getting that message. Anyway, I didn't have you two around to help me figure out how to handle it, and I made a bad choice.

I did some thinking about how tired I was of having this continue to happen and I remembered something dad had once told me. As you two are aware, dad is not a big man, but dad is tough, and it seems fair to say that *nobody messes with dad.* Well, dad once told me that, "The bigger they are, the harder they fall." So, after church one Sunday afternoon I went up to Jay on the sidewalk outside and acted like I was really glad to see him. He said, "Hi, Carson," and I said "Hi, Jay," back to him, and then I told him I was impressed with the double he hit last summer in the church softball game against One-Way Baptist. I could tell he appreciated the compliment and I could see him re-imagining that moment in his mind—the beautiful hit he had made to left center field that drove in two runs allowing our team to finally take the lead. Then, when he was distracted with his thought processes and looking the other way, I kicked him as hard as I could, in the shin—he never saw it coming.

As I look back in time, I remember the experience as if in slow motion. I was in some ways shocked with the result of my action. He is so much bigger than me that I expected to have little impact, but his knees actually buckled and he went to the pavement. His face possessed a look of disbelief at what had just occurred. All of a sudden, I felt this strange sense of power. I ran home thinking I was the king of the world, and that he would give me no more Dutch Rubs. I was in a grand and elated mood...until mom and dad got home.

The look of disappointment in mom's eyes was incredible, and dad was very stern. He didn't spank me. Instead he had a talk with me. He said he could not believe I had done what I did; that I really could have hurt Jay. He pointed out that Bowser could have caught up with me and cleaned my clock had he decided to do so, and he said that *Bowser is probably the closest thing I have to an older brother...which I had not considered, but which indeed may now be true since you guys are gone.* I walked over to his house and apologized, and Jay forgave me. What a great guy Jay was to so quickly forgive me. He didn't make me beg, or anything. He just said that I was important to him, that it was okay, and that he forgave me... But I was not done with bad choices.

A few days later, as your birthdays were approaching, I got it in my head that I might somehow be able to send birthday cards to you two through the mail even though you are 50 years ahead of me. Isn't that nutty? But I convinced myself it might be possible. I thought I should surely enclose some type of gift for each of you so that evening I stole two dollars from dad's wallet and enclosed one in each of your cards. I know it was wrong, because Christians don't steal, but as I've already said, I haven't been myself lately. When dad discovered what I had done he was astounded. He spoke to me this time with a loud voice about the importance of being an honest person. Mom started crying. He seemed to get more upset when he saw mom crying and he said loudly "I am not going to have a son of mine be a thief." I was on the other side of the dining room table from dad, and in a really bad mood that evening. I looked him in the eyes and said, "What is an old man like you, with a bad back, going to do about it? Trade me in for a different son?"

I think you both would be very proud of dad, because everyone knows dad can be pretty tough. He went stone silent and simply told me to go to bed, which I did. The next day he spoke with me and explained that he had scheduled an appointment for me to speak with Reverend Warner at the church office. He recommended that I speak with Reverend Warner about whether I intended to become a thief and why I had treated Jay Bowser as I had. He let me know two days later that he had arranged for me to work for eight hours at the church on the next two Saturdays, with Sam Longacre and Don Ross, doing things to clean and fix the church. He said I probably needed a consequence for some of my recent unfortunate choices.

Mr. Longacre and Mr. Ross did give me a lot of work to do. They kept me busy, but they were also very kind. I don't think I'll tell dad but working with those two guys was in some ways great. They know how to fix so many things and they did not criticize me for the bad things I had done.

When I met with Reverend Warner, dad stipulated that I pay to the church one of my beloved silver dollars in order to pay for the minister taking his time with me. Pastor Warner was very polite, and thoughtful and respectful. He said these behaviors of mine had taken him by surprise. He mentioned that he had never seen a member of our family behave in this manner. He said *he is certain that God is willing to forgive me, but that God has given us all free will, and thus in time I will be the primary person who will decide who I am going to become, how I will behave, and for instance, whether I will be a thief.* His advice gave me some important things to consider. Yet I still was not done with causing problems.

In the past I had always prided myself on being one of the best-behaved students at McCormick Elementary School. Always pretty good grades, polite to others, and never behavior problems. But about three weeks after I stole the money from dad, I decided it would be a good idea to start making weird noises in class when Mrs. Snowden's back was turned toward the chalk board. Dogs barking...cats meowing...and I do a pretty good cow. It took her the better part of a week to figure out it was me because I was someone she never suspected. When she finally caught me, she was flabbergasted. She sent me to the Principal's office, and mom was called to pick me up.

That evening mom and dad both seemed bewildered. Dad didn't spank me and mom didn't cry. They both told me that they just did not understand what was going on, and that they agreed with Mr. Buel Smith, the Principal, that I should see the School Counselor. An appointment was arranged for me the following Tuesday.

The Counselor was polite and good at listening. I decided to take a chance and told her my whole story—that I had had two terrific and amazing twin brothers, six years older than me, and one day they just disappeared and no one besides me even remembered them. (I decided not to tell her about the cell phone). She was quite surprised at the very detailed stories I told her about so many of the fun things we had done together over the years. I even told her about the time I got mad at Larry in a football game and jumped on his back to attack him as if I was bigger than him. She asked if Larry continued to like me after that incident and I said, "Sure, it didn't change our relationship at all; that's how our family is. We care about each other."

We only had one session together but what she said did help. *She told me she thought I was grieving.*
I responded that I thought grieving was only when people die.

She said no, that we grieve any time we lose someone, sometimes when we lose something important to us, and certainly when we lose a relationship. She said that if I really believe I used to have two older brothers then recognizing I no longer have them is clearly a loss and she said she was very sorry for the emotional pain I was experiencing. Since I am absolutely positive that you guys used to be a part of my life, I realized she was right. It was okay to feel sad and given time I would probably get better. That was a month ago and my behaviors seem back to normal for the most part.

By the way, I got to thinking that I have seen both of you in these movies in the future, but I have not seen myself. Perhaps something happens to me in the next 50 years—I cannot be sure. *I can't be certain who I will be in the future nor how much time in the future I have, but I think probably it is important that I should focus on being the best guy I can be in the now.*

I hope you two are doing okay 50 years in the future. I'm still worried about you having a bully for a President, and one who seems to lie a lot, but maybe I'll write more another time about those concerns and questions. I still check under the loose board on the front porch railing at least twice a week. If this house is still here 50 years in the future maybe it would work for you to leave a message for me there.

I hope you two are okay.

Your brother,

Carson

THE IMPORTANCE OF FORGIVENESS

Letter Three

April 5, 1967

Dear Larry and Harry,

It's been almost two weeks since I last wrote to you. I know you probably are not getting these letters, but I guess I need to write them. After all, it was a pretty big thing for me when you disappeared in late November, and the fact that no one else even remembers you makes the situation all the worse. My school counselor told me she thinks I am grieving and it is really hard to grieve when you can't talk with anyone about the loss.

I've been to several funerals at the church and I remember when Grandpa died... I have always noticed that the person who loses the loved one cannot stop talking about what has happened. Everyone around the person respectfully and politely listens to the story of how the person died and how the loved one found out about it, again and again, as many times as the person feels they need to say it. Perhaps talking about the loss is one of the main ways that people grieve. Perhaps writing these letters is my way of talking about my loss. I told my story of you two disappearing, in detail, to mom three times, but I had to stop. Each time I told her, I could see that she was getting more and more concerned. I could see in her eyes that she was worried about me. She must have thought understandably that her son was going nuts. So now when she asks me if I still worry about the older brothers I think I lost, I lie to her. I tell her "It must have been a really strange dream. It was a dream that seemed so very real at the time, but I am over it now and don't think about it much." I hope it's not a sin to lie to mom about this. I never intended to become a liar.

I cannot ask my Sunday School teachers about whether it is okay to lie to mom about my situation because I am certain that out of concern for me the teacher would feel the need to tell mom and dad, and then mom would again be worried. I guess there are some things in this life you have to figure out how to handle on your own. Uncle Ray once told me that. I kept getting my fishing line caught in weeds, fishing on the Camp Koinonia lake from off the bridge, even after both he and dad had warned me it is very easy to get your line caught in the weeds there. After he saw me struggle with the problem the third time, he did not criticize me. He simply said, *"There are some things in life people have to figure out for themselves."* After he made this comment, I promptly took my fishing pole and went to fish off the dam.

I guess the main thing I want to talk about today is *forgiveness*. I mainly want to say that *it works*. If you saw my second letter you will surely understand that forgiveness was something that I was needing a lot of about six weeks ago, but it has worked out pretty well for me. Jay Bowser forgave me. I already told you that when I apologized for kicking him so hard and unexpectedly, he told me he forgave me, but I wondered would he really be able to. What I did was pretty far out of line. I would not have blamed him if he couldn't have forgiven me, and even after he said he would I didn't really count on it. But he has been amazing. He has in many ways begun to act like the older brother that he assumes I have never had. He is not as good as you guys, but who could be?

Mrs Snowden has forgiven me a lot faster than I expected. The school counselor recommended I make an apology to her and I asked Mrs. Snowden if I could apologize to her in front of the entire class and she said okay. I told her I knew it was a mistake to make those animal sounds during class when she was facing the chalk board and that with her being the great teacher she is, she did not deserve this, and that I was sorry. There is really only one kid in my class who doesn't like me—Danny. Danny said after my apology statement, "What are you going to do, Carsonbaby, cry?" I looked at him, with just a touch of fire in my eyes, and said, "Maybe," but then I didn't. Mrs. Snowden gave a stern look to Danny, and then looked at me, and said that my apology was one of the best she had ever received and that it was accepted. She also commented that I do a remarkably good imitation of a cow, to which I said thank you. I have since worked each day to make her life as a teacher a little easier.

Honestly, the *hardest apology* was to dad. I asked myself a hundred times why I got mad and called dad an old man with a bad back. Why was I so rude? The next day, our younger brother, Ray, told me he was angry with me that I had said such a mean thing to dad, and in time I realized that Ray had every right to be mad. We are taught at church to honor our father and mother and I was not even close that evening to following what the Bible says. But apologizing to dad is not the easiest thing in the world—I'm not certain whether this is because of who he is or because of who I am.

Several days after I said the mean things to dad, I found him in the converted chicken house that he uses as a workshop in the far part of our back yard. At first, I climbed the mulberry tree near the back corner of the chicken house and sat on top of it for a while, all the time aware that I was avoiding something—that I really did not want to talk with dad about what I had done. Finally, I went inside and told dad I was sorry for the way I had treated him. He asked me "Why?" I was puzzled at his response and said, "Why what?" He said, "Why are you sorry you said those mean things to me?" I thought about it for a brief time. Then I explained to him that I had been having a really bad time for a while, and I was really mad, and like him, I was upset that I had made mom cry, but that I was sorry because he did not deserve the mean things I had said. He thought about my response for a moment and then said it was okay. He said he had done some really numb-skull things himself in earlier days. Just try not to do it again. I told him thanks, and that was it.

I suppose the message of this letter is that forgiveness really is important, and that if you do forgiveness right, it can make a difference. It can really work. You guys already know this, but I didn't. When I think about the time you two are in, 50 years ahead of me, I still worry about how things are going. From watching the movies I have watched (many times now) I am hoping your new President has asked for forgiveness of many people. If he has, I think the people in our country are by and large pretty forgiving people, like the people who have recently forgiven me.

I hope he has asked forgiveness of Jeb Bush for calling him Low Energy Jeb, and Marco Rubio for calling him Little Marco. I hope he has asked forgiveness of Senator Cruz for insinuating that his father had something to do with assassinating JFK—that seems pretty crazy. I hope he has apologized to the previous President for saying he wasn't born in the United States just because he is black. That must have offended many people. I especially hope he has apologized to that nice Muslim couple, Mr. and Mrs. Khan. After all, they surely had a right to speak out and express their opinions about our country given the reality that their son was a hero who gave his life so that his friends could live, like we believe Jesus did for us. *I hope he has asked for a whole lot of forgiveness. If not, I am worried about how things might be going in your world.*

I know you probably don't get these letters but I want you to know I still remember you both.

Your brother,

Carson

UNUSUAL DEVELOPMENTS

Letter 4

May 16, 1967

Dear Larry and Harry,

I hope you both are doing well in 2017. I'm still stuck in 1967. The two of you disappeared the day after Thanksgiving 1966, and in this universe, I am the only person who remembers you. Sometimes there is a part of me that wants to believe I have just made up the fantasy that I had two older, terrific twin brothers who all the time did so many neat and fun things with me, that it is...just my imagination, running away with me...but then I snap back to reality. I know the truth. You two were here and now you are not.

When I watched the Star Trek episode this past October of Spock getting caught in a Time Warp, which put him into a parallel universe, I thought the episode was interesting, but I certainly did not think it could be real. I'm a believer now, and that is for sure. A few weeks ago, I heard Ronnie and Robbie, two of the best students at McCormick elementary school talking about Einstein. Ronnie said that in his theory, Einstein spoke about the flexibility of the space/time continuum.

Flexibility of the space/time continuum? What the heck might that even mean? I thought space was space and time was time. How could they possibly be put together? But, Einstein was surely on to something with his theory and I was all ears for what they had to say, and they cannot possibly know why I was listening so intently. I feel certain they have never lost anyone they cared for to a different universe, nor of course how painful that can be. Now let me be clear, I still have a really good life as an 11-year-old guy here in Wichita—some would say a great life. Its just different without the two of you, with a definite element of sadness, but no one can understand that other than me.

Today has been a beautiful day in Wichita. I really like springtime in Kansas. The huge elm trees in our yard are in full leaf. They are just begging to be climbed. I would bet a lot of money that kids will be climbing these wonderful trees in our yard hundreds of years from now—they are so amazing. The sky has been abundantly blue the last several days. The temperature in the past week has hit 80 several times. It has been pretty nice.

I apologize for how long it has been since I last wrote to you (April 5). I have been pretty busy. Mrs. Snowden came up with the idea of a social studies/history class project on the topic: "Extraordinary People from Kansas." Everyone in the class was to write a report about one of our extraordinary citizens and then we were to compile it into a giant report—basically a small book. In front of the entire class Mrs. Snowden complimented me about my interests in history and social studies and my developing writing skills, and then she asked me if I would be willing to be the Chief Compiler of this important class project. How do you refuse something like that? After an awkward pause, I stood up and said sure, that I would be willing to do this—the entire class clapped for me. Then I sat down and said to myself, "Oh boy. I was hoping to play a lot of softball this spring."

The class project has indeed been a lot of work. An awful lot of work. I have done some thinking about why Mrs Snowden selected me for this project. I have come to secretly suspect it may have had something to do with my brief but quite significant period of classroom misbehaviors this past winter. In case you did not see letter two, I was having some personal problems and for several days I decided it would be a good idea to make animal sounds when Mrs. Snowden was facing the chalk board. It took her several days to catch me, and of course it was not one of my proudest moments. If I were to provide a name for this class project, perhaps it should be, "Pretty Worthwhile Social Studies Project Developed to Keep Carson Busy this Spring so that He Does Not Have Time to Mess Up Again." Fortunately, I finished it yesterday. My buddies, Ronnie and Robbie, the really great students I mentioned earlier, offered significant assistance for which I am grateful.

There are a few other things currently going on with me in Mrs. Snowden's class. I think I mentioned in letter two that there is a kid in the class with whom I do not get along well. His name is Danny. He is about 5 inches taller and 40 to 50 pounds heavier than I and he is strong. He has decided it is kind of fun to mess with me. Sometimes he calls me names, though never within earshot of a teacher. When we pass each other on the sidewalk he likes to bump into me and say "excuse me" but it is clear he doesn't mean it. Occasionally he jumps suddenly into a ninja posture and makes a weird yell and acts as if he is ready to provide me with a deadly karate chop. It is so annoying.

Danny does seem like he is probably a pretty tough cookie, though I rather doubt he has had training in Karate. I honestly don't know why he took a disliking for me, but unfortunately now the feeling is mutual. Why is it that sometimes two guys seem to, for some unknown reason, just not like each other? And, why is it that sometimes some guys think it's fun to pick on and bully others? I think perhaps Danny thought that since I try to be a nice guy most of the time, and since I am smaller than him, I would simply slink away if he messed with me. The problem is that for some reason I'm not good at slinking, I guess. Perhaps I am being prideful, and some say that pride is a sin, or that pride can easily cause a person to sin. I've heard dad say that "pride cometh before a fall," which I believe may come from the book of Proverbs.

This Danny difficulty is one of those things where I wish I had you guys around to help me figure out what the heck to do (sorry, maybe I'm not supposed to say the word, heck; one of you once commented that it is just two letters away from saying a word that is clearly out of line). Anyway, I talked with my Sunday school teacher about the situation with Danny and she said that in the Bible, Jesus tells us to turn the other cheek and to try to be forgiving. She asked me whether maybe Danny has problems at home. Perhaps he has a mean dad, or something. I told her I didn't know what his home life is like, nor whether he has a mean dad, and I thanked her for her ideas.

Next, I talked with Phil Ruger about what he might do in a situation like this, with Danny. His advice was, let's say…, a little bit different from the advice I received from my Sunday school teacher. Or I guess I could go ahead and admit it was almost polar opposite. I don't think I'll tell you exactly what Phil suggested, but I will say that I think he cares about me and is genuinely trying to look out for my best interests. I could tell by his facial expression that he did not like it when I described how Danny was treating me. Frankly, I don't like it one bit either. One thing Phil asked me was whether I am afraid of Danny with him being so much bigger, and stronger. I honestly told him I am not afraid. The truth is that you two, and dad, and maybe Uncle Ray and a few others, have all taught me there is no need most of the time in life to be afraid. I am frustrated with Danny, and I am befuddled, but I am definitely not afraid. I'm just not sure what to do. Anyway, don't worry about me. I'm sure I will work this out, one way or the other.

So, back to my main story for today...I've been sending my letters to the two of you assuming my messages go into thin air and then several days ago something very unusual occurred. In the world of unusual developments, it doesn't get a lot more unusual than this one.... As normal, I turned on the cell phone by pressing a button. Then I put in the pass code, which happens to be your birthday (for both of you, of course). I went to the section entitled Messenger. I wanted to read my previous letter that I had written to you—and there it was--*a message back to me*.... Let me say it again to be clear...***I received a fricking return message!***

I was sitting at the top of the basement stairs to open the cell phone to read from it, and I was so startled when I saw the return message, that I fell halfway down the stairs nearly injuring myself. I heard dad yell, "Are you okay down there?" "Yeah. I'm okay," I replied. "Sorry. I just tripped." To say I was shocked is definitely an understatement. The message was short and simple. It said just three words, "*Take it easy*." I was completely freaked out.

I didn't sleep a wink the night I found the message, which was unfortunate since I had a math test in Mrs. Snowden's class the next day. When she returned my exam, she commented that she thought I knew my math facts much better than that. I commented that I too was surprised by the situation in which I found myself.

By the end of the first day after receiving the message, I was almost convinced perhaps it was from one or both of you, but over time it just didn't make sense. If you guys were responding you surely would have said more. You likely would have tried to answer some of my questions from letter one. You might have said that you were pleased I had my behavior back in line (letter two). You would have likely told me you were impressed and pleased that Jay Bowser was a good enough guy to truly forgive me for kicking him (letter three). You would surely have asked me how the other family members were doing in this parallel universe. I decided in the end, the message could be from one or both of you but it seemed improbable.

Then I got to thinking Phil Ruger was maybe messing with me. He could have gone to the Messenger section of the phone, and read some of my letters, and written a return message just to freak me out. I gave that possibility some serious consideration but, in the end, concluded no. Phil just does not seem to be a guy who plays a lot of practical jokes. I think he understands how important this cell phone is to me, though I don't think he understands why. He finds the movies entertaining but assumes they are fantasy. He has not yet seen anyone he knows, like I have. He always gives me the phone on Wednesday evenings at church (with no one watching) and I return it to him Sunday evenings. Occasionally, if he wants me to, I walk it over to his house or his parents' Laundry Mat. By the way, I have done some additional thinking about how in the world Phil came up with this cell phone. I mean, think of it, it comes from 50 years in the future. It is hard to draw a conclusion other than the idea that Phil may have connections with a Time Traveler, or someone who knows a Time Traveler. It makes my head hurt to think about the possibilities.

My next line of reasoning perhaps seems unusual, and I hesitate to even admit to it, but for two or three days I became convinced that the message may have been from God. I mean, there is a song at church that declares that God pays such attention to detail in our world that..."His eye is on the sparrow"...so if God is concerned even about each and every sparrow in our world, surely he knows what the last few months have been like for me.

I mean, ...having two terrific older brothers disappear and then no one else remembering them at all is not the worst thing in the world, because I believe you guys are okay 50 years in the future...but it is not the easiest thing either. Perhaps this was a message from God that I should "take it easy" and calm down.

I got to thinking about some of the Bible stories from Sunday School in which God spoke with people. Then I did some looking into examples in the Bible. In Genesis, chapter 3, it pretty clearly states that God actually talked with Adam, and then with Eve, and it sounds like he probably used a human voice.

By the way, that cannot have been a good day for Adam as it was described in chapter 3. Not only did Adam eat from one of the trees God distinctly told him not to eat from, but then he said essentially to God that it wasn't his fault; that Eve caused him to do it. Wow! No wonder God kicked him out of the garden. I mean, I've done some numb-skull things before, but that one takes the cake. I would bet that later, Adam was saying to himself, "I should have stood up and taken my punishment like a man. Instead I came across to the Almighty like a real wimp. I guess its a good thing I didn't react with my first inclination. I was tempted to tell God that I'm pretty sure I suffer from a history of poor parenting and that this is the reason I messed up. Then, fortunately it came to me that God actually created me...I have no parents... Wow!... At least I didn't make that excuse. Thank heavens for small blessings." But I guess my point is that God spoke (apparently in a voice) to both of them.

In the sixth chapter of Genesis, once again God spoke with someone--this time it was Noah. He let him know he was not pleased with how people were behaving in the world and essentially God said he thought it would be a good idea for Noah to build a very large ark, because a lot of rain would soon be coming. He spoke with Noah, apparently again in a voice. I wonder if Noah told anyone he was hearing a powerful voice, and how awkward that might have been. "Hey, Jacob, guess who I heard from today?... Yeah, you are right. It was God. How did you guess?... No, God didn't say that. He told me to build the biggest boat ever... Yeah, I know we don't live on a lake. But, between you and me, I think I'm going to start working on getting the lumber ready. You want to help? Oh, I see. I guess you do have a pretty big flock of sheep, and you have your three wives to look after. No, I understand." I mean, what might people have thought if Noah had admitted to his buddies he had heard directly from God? Do you think perhaps they might have considered him somewhat strange?

I don't mean to go on too much about the Noah thing, but I do think it would have been honestly weird to have God telling you, in a voice, to build an amazingly large boat, unless you happen to live in a very low lying area near the sea, and there is nothing in the story to indicate this was the case. Last spring I did some discussing of just this issue with my buddies, Leon Knolte and Clark Ginn, after mom led our Sunday School lesson on the topic of Noah and the Ark (mom was our teacher this past school year). I was asking them how in the world one would have the confidence to trust that you were hearing God and that you were not simply going nuts? Clark was getting one of those unusual expressions where it really seems his whole face grins, yet very slyly. He says so much with his face. Leon, on the other hand, has almost no facial expression and then he can shock you with a comment or observation that you would simply never expect, which was indeed the case that day.

Leon pointed out that Noah was pretty doggone old when God spoke to him and told him to build the ark. I asked what the heck that had to do with anything. Then he sprung it on me— he said that Noah lived to be 950 years of age, to which I immediately said, "No way; not a chance!" Then he picked up a Bible and turned to Genesis 9:29, and sure enough he was right. Leon, as only Leon can say it, with no emotional expression whatsoever, went on to explain that according to the Bible, Noah's first son was born when he was 500, that the flood came along at about 600 years, and that therefore God must have spoken to Noah to give him his important assignment at maybe 550 years of age. He went on to suggest that a person can surely develop a whole lot of wisdom in 500 years of life experiences, and that this would perhaps have helped him with discerning that he wasn't going nuts, and that God really and truly was talking to him. Leon sure gave me something to think about that day, but back to my main point here. Even if Noah was of a very advanced age, what might people have thought if Noah had admitted to those he knew that he had heard God speaking to him? He might have certainly received some very strange looks.

You surely know where I am going next. In the third chapter of Exodus...God spoke to Moses, this time from the midst of a burning bush--*A freaking burning bush!* That must have been crazy! But I have to give this one to Moses. He handled it incredibly. When God told him it would be a good idea to take his shoes off because he was walking on holy ground Moses didn't bat an eye. He took his shoes off immediately, stayed calm and respectful, and listened to all the various things God had to say to him. Moses was clearly the man! You have to admit, to a certain extent, Moses kind of made Adam not look so good in comparison. I think he made Adam look like a bit of a whiner. But that is beside the point. The point is...God once again spoke with someone, and with a voice. So, anyway, I hope you guys don't think its too weird that for a few days, I mean to tell you—I was convinced God had written the message—but then what was the meaning? I could not figure out what he was trying to tell me. "Take it easy." What a vague and unusual message.

Then I finally figured out what likely had occurred. I concluded I had a spy in my midst...A wonderful, beautiful, brilliant, speed-reading spy who got almost all A's at Wichita West High School and mainly A's in college as well, and who was trying to look out for me and my best interests—and I think you know who it was. Yes, you are correct. The message appeared the week that our older sister, Sara, was home for Spring Break from Morrison College in Morrison, Indiana. Once I thought of this possibility, I was pretty sure I had it right. My wonderful older sister, like a second mom to me, had invaded my privacy, found the phone, somehow figured out how it worked and had read my letters to the two brothers she thinks I have imagined. At first, I was outraged! My privacy had been invaded. How could she do this to me?

But, after I thought about it for a while, I thought of the reality that by golly, this was Sara. For my whole life, like you guys, she has only looked out for my well-being. She had doubtlessly heard from mom and dad about my period of terrible behavior problems. I think she probably searched my room to see if she would find beer, or marijuana, or some other type of drugs. Instead she found the doggone phone. I am just thankful she didn't tell mom and dad about it. She read my letters (very quickly no doubt), and wrote a simple message that probably isn't bad advice..."Take it easy"...and she put the phone back in the secret place where I keep it, under the basement stairway, not far from the sump pump, behind a board.

So, I have been thinking about her message, or perhaps I am wrong and one of you somehow sent me the message. I am totally convinced it was not a message from God. I'm not nearly that important. And, I really don't think it was a practical joke.

I had by that point in time calmed down with my behavioral problems. Maybe the message was that I could calm down a bit more with some of what I say in these letters. And maybe I need to be aware that since my privacy felt invaded, perhaps yours could too, if somehow these letters get through to the two of you.

Maybe these letters are getting through to you, and maybe you are not the only ones who can read them. That could be weird.

So, going forward I think I'll try to be a bit calmer about the way I say some of the things I say. (After all, some of the questioning at the end of the first letter was rather pointed). And, I think maybe I should address these letters to other names. It might not be appropriate that I continue to use your names. It could be an invasion of your privacy. I'll maybe experiment with other twin names or simply names I like that seem to go together. I may use several sets of names before I find the ones I like. I know it is possible that you may not find my letters if they are not addressed to you, but if you really want to find them you probably can. Just look for letters addressed to names you think I might like.

And, frankly, I am aware at this point that I am probably writing these letters more for me than for you. I have been through quite a saga and it helps me to get my words out in print, and even to re-read my thoughts. It kind of clarifies for me how I think of things and how I want to think of things, and how I think of life, and how I want to think of life. So there may be future letters but this letter will likely be the last one addressed directly to the two of you. I think it might be better that way.

I hope you guys are okay. You are, by the way, the best brothers.

Your brother,
Carson

THE LEGEND OF
TALL TALE TONY

Letter 5

July 1, 1967

Dear Wilbur and Orville,

I sent my last letter to you on May 16. I hope you both are doing well 50 years in the future. I also hope you like the new names I have selected. I promised I would select new names in letter 4 and I gave my reasons as well. I am not sure if I will stay with these names but I am partial to them since, of course, family legend has it that our great grandfather knew the grandfather to Wilbur and Orville Wright. I have heard that both men were United Brethren Ministers.

What an incredible accomplishment those two brothers made in the sand hills of North Carolina. It's hard to believe that the first flight ever was only 64 years ago. It boggles my mind. When I consider that our family had some kind of connection, however minor, to one of their family members, it makes the world seem strangely small--which is of course is what airplanes also are doing. There is a sign at the Wichita city limits that says, "Wichita, Air Capitol of the World." I suppose that is because we manufacture so many airplanes in Wichita. The Wright Brothers' invention has clearly had a huge impact on our world here in south central Kansas.

The weather here has been nice. We have had a reasonable amount of rain this summer as Kansas summers go and thus the huge elm trees in our yard are doing well. They are a lot of fun to climb.

School has been out for quite a while. I have been mentioning to you in earlier letters the trouble I was having with one of the kids in my class this past year. Indeed, I had trouble with Danny to almost the very end of the school year. He kept looking for opportunities to make disrespectful comments that I would hear, and to some of my friends as well, but always out of earshot of Mrs. Snowden. He continued to jump into his ninja posture at odd times, as if to threaten me, and he would sometimes let out a loud ninja screech. It was very annoying. Sometimes he would bump into me on the sidewalk. It became unclear to me what I might do to respond other than move things in a direction I did not really want to go.

I did some additional talking with another of my past Sunday School teachers and received some of the earlier advice I have mentioned. I also talked more with Phil Ruger about his experience with such situations. He had plenty to say, though his commentary did continue to conflict quite a bit with my Sunday School teacher's advice. But, anyway, the Danny thing is done. I don't feel like talking about it yet. It ended up rather complicated and I am still trying to figure out how I think about what finally occurred, how I behaved, and so on. It didn't really happen in quite the way I might have predicted, but that has been my life recently.

After all, this past eight months has been nuts. You two disappeared the day after Thanksgiving, 1966, and in this universe, I am the only person who remembers you. I do not feel terrible about the situation, because in the movies I have watched on the cellphone brought to me by Phil (somehow, from 50 years in the future)--I believe I have seen you two and you are still okay--in the future. But, of course, the reality that you two are okay in the future offers only a certain amount of consolation. There is still an emptiness to deal with.

I have successfully stopped talking about the parallel universes to anyone, with one exception. I no longer talk about what happened this past November when I speak with mom--I saw the worry in her eyes when I would mention such things last winter. Dad is clearly not one to suffer fools, as they say, and I think that is how he would think of it if I were again to raise the issue. The one exception is that I have a church pen pal who lives in another state. I have shared with him the terrible loss I experienced last Fall. Remarkably, he has remained supportive and has not become judgmental. He also promised he would tell my story to no one. This is the first pen pal I have ever had. It seems really odd to communicate with someone I have never actually met, and to begin to feel that he is in many ways my friend. How is it possible to be a friend with someone you have never actually met? I can't even call him because long distance phone calls are so expensive and it's hard to make money when you are only eleven.

Softball season is in full swing, and I have made an effort to go to every game of our church team—the Southwest Prairie Sluggers, even though it is still two years before I will be old enough to play. I think of you guys when I go to those games and I have always loved softball. The team has done remarkably well this season given that they lost two of the best players in the league (you guys) – but no one else understands that besides me. We did lose game one, to One-Way Baptist. I'm sure you remember those guys.

They talk of being such great Christians, but then when things don't go their way, they can sometimes be pretty quick to run you over even if you stay out of the baseline, and it seems that more of our players end up cleated somehow when playing against those guys. But I suppose that story can be left for another day.

After the loss to One-Way Baptist we went on a pretty decent winning streak. Phil Ruger missed the initial game but has been present for all the others. Game seven was quite a memorable game. We played a very good, previously unbeaten Pawnee Avenue Wesleyan church team, and managed to win 8 to 5. It was a very hard-fought game but without any of the One-Way Baptist shenanigans.

Our team was hitting on all cylinders that night, as they say, which by the way does not occur all too often these days with dad's 1957 Ford Fairlane station wagon, with the wood grain paneling on the side. At least according to dad, it is not always hitting on all cylinders. He has not recently been real happy with that car. I often hear him say that Ford stands for Fix Or Repair Daily. Like I say he has not been happy. But, where else can you buy a car? Ford, Chrysler and General Motors. I cannot think of any other reasonable possibilities. You are certainly not going to buy a car from a place like Japan. That is for sure. Maybe it is not especially nice but when any of my friends hear that something has been made in Japan, they kind of immediately start chuckling. Primarily trinkets and nonessential things are made there.

But back to the Pawnee Avenue game. The highlight was Phil's third at-bat in the fifth inning. Prior to the game the umpire brought the coaches together and explained that he was aware that the oak tree along the left field line was quite a ways out there, but that if a heavy hitter happened to hit a ball in fair condition into that tree, even though it seems unfair it would be treated as a ground rule double. Coach Mac Waters responded by

saying he didn't think anyone could possibly hit the ball that far.
The umpire said he agreed but he wanted everyone to be clear in
case this unlikely event should occur. By the way, why is it we
never play on any of the fancy fields with fences? And, why don't
our players have uniforms, like some of the other teams? That
might be nice.

Anyway, I guess nobody told Phil Ruger it wasn't possible to hit
the ball that far because he hit the doggone ball over the tree,
and it landed in fair territory and it rolled and rolled and rolled.
It was unbelievable! He rounded the bases at a slow trot wearing his shaded sunglasses and what looked like a very slight grin
on his face. Just after he stepped on third his brother, Rob, in a
show of brotherly support handed him an ice-cold bottle of coke
which Phil grabbed without breaking his stride. Then he stopped
ten feet from home plate and drank half of the coke at a leisurely
pace--he even belched out loud. He refused to look behind himself to see how close the ball was approaching. (He later told me
he was watching the catcher's eyes). Everyone started screaming
that he would be tagged out as the ball approached home plate.
It was very dramatic. At the last possible moment, he trotted
the final four steps and tagged home base just before the catcher
caught the ball. It was both amazing and hilarious. Phil kept the
same slight grin on his face the entire time but never cracked a
smile. The umpire said nothing.

I guess what Phil did is called "show-boating." I was previously
unfamiliar with the term. Whatever it was I hope someday I
have a chance to do something like that. It was pretty neat. I
think the showboating may have made Pastor Warner a slight
bit uncomfortable, as he was sitting in the stands. He may have
been concerned that the Pawnee Avenue folks might think people
from our church aren't considerate, compassionate and humble
Christians. I heard him go up to a man after the game who I think
may have been the minister. He said, "You know, I thought your

son, Chuck, made a fine double into left center field in the second inning this evening. You must have been very proud." The man responded by saying that indeed he was. Then Pastor Warner said, "I hope the show-boating that went on didn't come across as disrespectful." The other pastor was very gracious and said, "If I hit a ball like that, I just might do some show-boating myself."

By the way, how is it that Phil is able to do this kind of thing? I haven't seen any other hits like that one by anyone else this summer. Nor did I see anything like this in previous summers. It's just like that guy from Wichita East High school—Jim Ryun. Three years ago, as a high school Junior, he ran a mile in under four minutes. How did he do that? Are some people just different from the rest of us?

I am aware that I am off topic, so let me now get to the point. Today I want to talk some about an experience I had this past year in Sunday school at our church. Mom was our teacher and I thought she did a great job. Everyone really liked her and I'm sure you're not surprised about that. She only missed three classes the entire year, and one of those was the week Sara got married. That was one busy weekend. Anyway, I had a lot of friends in the class and we had quite a bit of fun. However, we had one continuing issue that for quite a while was a real struggle.

There was a new kid in class this year—his name was Tony. I would describe him as a pretty good-looking guy as fifth grade boys go. Brown hair, kind of tall, a solid build about him but not really heavy. He dressed nicely and came across as friendly and polite.

At first, I thought it was really neat having Tony in class. He had quite an interest in baseball and could quote baseball statistics like no one I have ever known. His favorite player was Willie Mays and his second favorite was Mickey Mantle--two excellent choices. Sometimes we would play Four Square after church on the sidewalk at the front of the building. He was very good. There were many good qualities about Tony, but in time it became clear he had one noticeable shortcoming...he liked to make things up.

It took me quite a while before I noticed the pattern. I think I tend to take at face value the things people tell me. Early on, I simply thought Tony was a really lucky fellow. He told me that his dad had purchased go-carts for him and his younger brother and that he had an Uncle who lived near Valley Center who had a go-cart track on his property. He went on to explain that except for the coldest days in winter he could ride his go-cart almost any time he wanted and basically for as long as he wanted. Let me state at this point, just for the record, that I am aware that one of the Ten Commandments says, "Thou shalt not covet." I am glad I am not completely certain what it means to covet, because I think I may have done a fair amount of that when Tony told me about his go-cart. I would think about how neat it would be to have a go-cart and to ride it as much as I wanted. Then I would be reminded that I had no such luxury in my life, which was somewhat painful. I was a bit surprised that he didn't invite any of us, his classmates, to go ride go-carts at his uncle's place, but I thought it would not be polite to ask. I just sat uncomfortably in my chair, coveting perhaps, when he would recount his stories.

A couple of weeks after his go-cart story, Tony shared one Sunday morning prior to class that the previous Friday evening he and his parents had attended the West High football game, a game by the way in which the West High Pioneers achieved a surprise win over South High with an interception and run back in the last minute of the game to put West High into first place in the City League. I wish to heck I had been there. Tony explained that he indeed was there, with very good seats, and that at the conclusion of this important game, three of the starters from the West High team sought him out in the stands to talk with him, a fifth grader, and to tell him that in a few short years they were very hopeful he would go out for the team because they had heard how great he is at football. Tony said they even introduced him to the head football coach. I don't know that I was guilty of coveting that morning. I think my emotional experience was one of good old-fashioned jealousy. Before class started, I asked my buddy, Leon Knolte, whether he thought it was a sin to be jealous. He said he had never thought about that, but then pointed out it is not in the Ten Commandments that--Thou shalt not be jealous. I thanked him for his input and breathed a sigh of relief.

The stories kept coming--a new one each week. I began to feel a slight bit of dread when I would see Tony, wondering what he might say next that would remind me that my otherwise pretty good life wasn't nearly quite as good as I might have been thinking. When just prior to Halloween, Tony told several of us about the two ponies his family had at their house, because they had a barn out back and a big enough yard for horses, I started to become suspicious. It all seemed just too good to be true. How could one kid possibly be so lucky? When he told his story of the two ponies, I saw Michael McDowell's eyebrows go up in a look of either surprise or disbelief—I could not tell which. Michael, as you may know is very quick thinking, and so he asked Tony, "Oh yeah? What are their names?" Tony hesitated, but quickly said, "Heckel and Jeckel," which are of course the names of two crows on a cartoon we all watch on Saturday mornings. Michael responded by saying, "Well, that's really neat," but I saw an interesting look in Michael's face.

Tony started bragging a little less for a few weeks, perhaps thinking we might be on to him, but in time he went back to his old ways. Each week he would have another amazing story. Michael's eyebrows would go up; Clark Ginn, one of my other close buddies, would get this astounded look on his face; and me, I suppose I started looking slightly irritated. By the way, I think Clark Ginn does the astounded look better than anyone I have ever seen. He gets this look that emotionally he is stuck somewhere between shocked and surprised, and yet you also can't tell what he is really thinking. You can just never know what he is thinking, and yet you are pretty sure something is going on in that head of his. Mom has been known to say about people like Clark that "still waters run deep." I guess that describes him best.

But back to me and my developing reaction, it just bugged me that Tony kept saying these things. If they were true, then life was absolutely unfair, and if they weren't true, this entire process was starting to feel bothersome, irritating, and even disrespectful. What did he take us for? Idiots? Why would he continue to say these outlandish things? This complicated situation became simply too much for me to properly cope with one Sunday morning shortly before Christmas.

I need to take a moment to explain that one of my very favorite things about being a member at Southwest Prairie Church is our production each year of Christ's Living Nativity. It has been going on now for several years. The men of the church put up a stable each winter shortly after Thanksgiving in the gravel and grass parking lot behind the church (the lot that during the summer serves as a great space for softball batting practice). After the stable is up, an area for the animals is fenced in. About 10 days before Christmas, a half dozen sheep and a donkey are brought in for the pageant. The ladies of the church put together the wardrobes--for Mary and Joseph, the Three Wise Men, Angel Gabriel, the Shepherds and shepherd boys (and shepherd girls too, I think).

For the week before Christmas the entire church is involved in putting on the re-enactment of Jesus' birth story. The music and narration is on the loud speaker which they attach to the telephone pole that stands right behind the stable. There are several presentations of the Christmas story each evening. Most years I have been able to play a shepherd boy role one or two evenings. You get as much hot chocolate as you want in Fellowship Hall in between performances. Then you return to your role in the enactment. It is often pretty cold on those December nights, but being a part in the presentation makes a person feel kind of important, like you are a part of something bigger than yourself. It is pretty neat.

I've been looking forward to getting older and getting to play Angel Gabriel, or one of the Wise Men. Thus, on the Sunday before Christmas, when Tony arrived early for class and shared with several of us his big news, it caught me off guard. He proudly and confidently announced that for Christmas Eve and Christmas night, he/Tony had been selected to play the role of Joseph!

I could not believe what my ears had just heard. I was aware that Tony was tall for a fifth grader and was indeed as tall as a few of the shorter men in the church. But, no fifth grader had ever, ever been selected to play Joseph. No one in junior high or high school had ever been selected to play Joseph. I don't really think any college students had ever been allowed the honor of playing Joseph. This statement was beyond the pale. Joseph? Joseph! This was ridiculous!

After Tony made his confident assertion, there was a remarkable moment of absolute silence. Michael, Clark, and I all looked at one another, at first with no expression on our faces. I would look at Michael, then at Clark, and they would do the same...shifting back and forth... Then it was if the dam had burst. We all broke out laughing at once, and I spontaneously pronounced... *"Your name cannot be Tony. Surely your name should be `Tall Tale Tony!'"* Everyone began to laugh, and it was one of those times of laughter where the experience became contagious. We would try to stop laughing, thinking the Sunday school teacher (our mom) would soon be walking in, and then, at least for me, it was as if my body demanded I start again. My sides would begin to contract involuntarily. I would try to stop but then I would make the mistake of looking at Michael or Clark and they would break into a smile and we would go for another round of uncontrollable emotion. This was one of those moments when Clark's understated, astounded look didn't really save him, as he almost fell off his chair, he was laughing so hard. Leon arrived after the event had unfolded and started laughing simply at the fact that we all were laughing so hard. He said, "You guys have gone nuts!" I retorted, "I think by golly you are absolutely right."

The only person not laughing was poor Tony. He just stood there with an awkward look on his face. Fortunately, mom had gone to the storage closet to get some supplies just prior to Tony's arrival and announcement. By the time she returned to begin the class we were able (barely) to control our laughter. Mom said "Is something wrong?" We all replied "No" almost in unison and went forward with our Christmas lesson. I worked at taking deep breaths to regain my composure. I knew I needed to calm myself down, but I could not remember ever having laughed so hard.

The nickname stuck. From that point forward, Mike and I never again called him Tony. We called him either Tall Tale or Tall Tale Tony, or sometimes to be creative we called him 3T's or even Mr. T. It was quite a lot of fun and I surely thought he deserved this result. He had lied to me and to us so many times. Someone once told me—*you reap what you sow in life.* It seemed to me he had surely sown the seeds to earn his nicknames. We would still attempt to be nice to Tony on Sunday mornings, but going forward we had him on a short leash. If he would start into a story and it was seeming a bit farfetched, one of us would say, "What are you trying to tell me, Mr. T?" or something similar. We were pretty careful about not saying such things around mom. Mom is nice to everyone. I felt sure she would not want to join in with what clearly needed to be accomplished. I did not want to put up with any more of Tony's tall tales. We had invented the solution to the problem and it was working well. My only experience of slight discomfort was with my buddy, Clark. He liked to have as much fun as anyone. Why, after the first day of laughter, was he seldom joining in with the fun of keeping Tony in line? He would get a slight astounded look on his face but that was all. I couldn't figure it out. Michael and I were a perfect team, and some of the other classmates helped out as well. At first Tony seemed to think it was funny too, but in time I could tell it was getting under his skin.

The Sunday school year was past Valentine's Day and into the windy month of March. Our lesson that second Sunday in March was about David and Goliath, one of my favorite stories. I always loved how the small guy took down the big mean guy. David took down Goliath permanently, and Goliath surely deserved it. This is a story about the way life should occur, and in the case of David, it did. About halfway through our lesson there came a knock on the door and in walked Goliath—or at least at first I thought so. He was the tallest guy in the church—Ernie Ginn (Clark's dad of course). I thought mom had planned his entrance for effect, but then I noticed she was surprised. "Ernie," she said, "What can we do for you?" With his very deep voice he said, "Harriet, I was wondering if I might have a few words with your son, Carson, and with Michael McDowell?" She said, "Well, of course you can. Have they done something I should know about?" "I don't really think so," Ernie said. Michael and I stood and followed Mr. Ginn out of the classroom.

Why is it that sometimes life seems to be going along so smoothly, and then in an instant it can turn on you? Why is it that you sometimes think you have a situation handled perfectly and then someone points out to you another way of looking at your situation and you see it completely differently? I knew immediately what was up as we followed the biggest, tallest guy in the church out of the classroom and into the empty classroom across the hall. On my way out I glanced at Clark and thought to myself—now I know why Clark has not been joining in! Darn! I had not thought of the fact that Clark's mom was teaching the fourth graders next door. He clearly knew that in time the gig would be up and we would answer for our behaviors. Why had he not thought to warn us? *"Be sure your sin shall find you out."* That was the scripture verse that came to mind as I walked out of the classroom.

It didn't help that Michael and I have not yet had our growth spurts. We are not shrimps, and Michael is a bit taller than me, but if we were teenagers at least we would come up to Ernie's shoulders. We went to the empty classroom and sat on the opposite side of the table from Ernie. Because the chairs were small, for kids, it made Ernie look even bigger than the big guy he already is. I felt as if I was sitting across the table from the real Goliath. He looked enormous.

"Fellows, what is this I hear about Tall Tale Tony, Triple T, and Mr. T? I wasn't aware you had someone in your class with that name, so it leaves me a bit confused as to what is going on." There was of course a momentary and very uncomfortable silence, after which I began to explain that Tony was new to the class this year and that at first I had liked him quite a lot, but that he told so many astounding stories and in time it became clear that few of these stories could possibly be true, and that when he said he had been selected to play Joseph in the church's presentation of The Living Nativity we had simply had enough and decided to put a stop to it.

Mr. Ginn was actually very respectful in his response. He said he agreed that it must have been troubling to find that Tony was telling stories that over time clearly, we knew could not be true. He asked why we thought he was telling these farfetched stories.

I said I had no idea whatsoever. He said he could understand why we were reacting as we had, but that he needed to ask us to please consider some other manner of handling this situation since it seems quite possible that if Tony has a problem with not telling the truth he may need the church even more than most people. He asked whether we had talked with mom about this since she is our teacher and I acknowledged that this clearly would have been a good idea.

The next development again caught me by surprise. I mentioned to you earlier that Michael McDowell can be very quick. I have since realized that those who are very quick are a little less predictable.

My view of what was going on in the moment was that we had been caught and called out. We were being called to task. The error of our ways had been exposed. We hadn't meant to be out of line but "the road to you-know-where is sometimes paved with good intentions," at least that is what Grandma says (her favorite expression). My view was that now is the time for us to fall prostrate on our faces, so to speak, and beg for forgiveness. But then I saw Michael get a gleam in his eye, and even a certain fierceness, and get ready to say something back to Mr. Ginn. I wanted to shout, "No!" "Don't do it Michael! If you back-talk one of the nicest men in the church, we will both be in more trouble with our parents than you can shake a stick at." I was dumbfounded and wanted to say something but nothing came out. I think someone once told me this type of thing is called the "deer in the headlight" experience. I said nothing and awaited my uncertain destiny.

Then what Michael actually said was even more shocking than I had expected. He looked directly at Mr. Ginn, right exactly in the eyes, and said, "Sir, I just want you to know that this whole thing was completely my fault. I'm the one who came up with the nick names. I'm the one who started calling him Tall Tale Tony. Carson had almost nothing to do with it." This of course would have been wonderful had it been true, but the reality is it was not true at all...So, what do you do when a buddy falls on his sword like that for you? I was stunned...

I know you are hoping that next I'm going to tell you how I immediately corrected Michael's statement and explained to Mr. Ginn that it was me. I was the one who had coined the nicknames, Tall Tale Tony, and Triple T and Mr. T, but once again I embraced the "deer in the headlight" experience. Ernie looked at me and sensed perhaps my moment of confusion. He said, "Did you have something to add to that, Carson?" That was clearly my moment to correct the record, but I was still in shock. Once again, I tried to speak but no words were uttered.

Then I finally just said, "No. Sorry." In time I managed to say, "Are you going to need to tell our parents? I understand if you do."

"I don't think so," said Ernie. "I trust you two young men to do your best to do the right thing going forward. Just keep in mind that Jesus taught us to love everyone. Even those who at times make our lives difficult." "Okay," I said, and then Michael agreed as well. Then I asked one more question, "Is Mrs. Ginn upset with us?" (She was someone both Michael and I liked a lot). "Heavens no," said Ernie. "She just wants things to turn out well for everyone." "Okay," I responded, and relieved I was.

Going forward we stopped with the name calling. It had been fun while it lasted but Mr. Ginn made a good point. If Tony had a problem, perhaps he needed the church even more than some of the rest of us, and I honestly thought that everyone needed the church.

After that, Tony and I did not become great friends but we got along. When school got out his family moved to El Dorado. His father got a job at the refinery there.

So that is my story of Tall Tale Tony. The experience was uncomfortable for a good while; then it was pretty fun for a period of time; and then it ended in a way that I would not have predicted. I'm not sure I'll ever forget the experience. So, what did I learn from it?

First of all, if you have a buddy like Michael McDowell, don't ever forget that he is your buddy. Friends like that don't come around every day. It felt to me like we were almost certain to be in big time trouble and he took all the blame on himself. That was an amazingly brave and strong thing to do. His action was incredible and honorable.

I learned that when you have a buddy who understates things, or as mom says, where "still waters run deep," it is not a bad idea to pay attention to what they might be trying to communicate.

I learned about the deer in the headlight experience. I really hope that as my life goes forward and I get older, that when I hit tough moments that I don't expect, I will be more able to speak up when I need to and want to, and hopefully I will become a bit more quickly brave, like Michael was.

Frankly, I also learned it is really, really, really a problem when someone lies a lot. You get to a point where you can't trust anything the person says because they have lied so many times. I listen to stories dad tells mom about problems connected to his work at the bank. He had a boss who was lying. Actually, the boss was stealing. He was setting up loans at the bank in the name of a fake person who did not exist. The boss found a way to receive the loan money and then predictably the loan payments were never made because the fake person did not exist, nor did anyone live at the fake address listed on the loan papers. When dad's boss was caught, he was fired. I don't know if he went to jail. There was no way the owners and managers of the bank could ever again trust him. In my situation, it wasn't that big of a deal that Tony was telling his stories of go-carts and ponies--those stories actually hurt no one. But when adults in positions of power lie about important things, or when they lie a lot, to the point you cannot trust what they say, this must create huge problems. I cannot imagine the complexity and difficulty this must create.

I hope you two are well 50 years in the future. I think of you often.

Your brother,

Carson

EXTRAORDINARY PEOPLE

Letter Six

Part One

August 1, 1967

Dear Ike and Wilt,

I sent my last letter to you on July 1. I have a feeling this letter is going to take quite a while to write because I have so much to say. It may be in several installments. I hope you are doing well 50 years in the future. I also hope you like the names I have selected for you for this letter. I selected these names from the class project we completed this past year in Mrs. Snowden's class; "Extraordinary People from Kansas." I thought I would begin this letter with accounts from two of my favorite Kansans drawn from the class project.

Dwight D. Eisenhower, affectionately known as "Ike" Eisenhower, was our 34th President, serving from 1953 through 1960. He was born on October 14, 1890, in Denison, Texas. He was the third of seven boys born to his parents. His father had owned a general store in Hope, Kansas, prior to Ike's birth, but the business failed and the family moved to Texas. They returned to Kansas in 1892 when Dwight was two, with 24 dollars to the family name. They moved to Abilene which became Ike's hometown. His father worked as a railroad mechanic and later at a creamery. As a young person growing up, Dwight had quite an interest in outdoors and hunting and fishing and card playing. He hunted and fished quite a lot along the Smokey Hill River.

His parents, it is said, believed in discipline and order, and daily family Bible reading. His mother was at one time a member of the River Brethren sect of the Mennonite Church, but she later became a part of the International Bible Students Association, which in time became known as the Jehovah's Witnesses. The Eisenhower family home served as a Meeting Hall for the Jehovah's Witnesses for nearly 20 years beginning in the mid 1890's, though Ike never formally joined this group. From what I could tell in my reading, it appears Ike considers himself a Christian. He was baptized in a Presbyterian church in 1952 at the age of 60. However, I suspect he may not be an Evangelical, like us. His love for playing poker, smoking, and a fair amount of reported drinking at times, seems rather inconsistent with my understanding of an Evangelical viewpoint.

Ike was accepted into West Point as a young man and then embarked upon his military career. He tried out for the baseball team at West Point and did not make it. That must have been disappointing. However, he did make the varsity football squad and it is said that he once tackled Jim Thorpe of the Carlisle Indians. Dwight injured his knee in a football game and re-injured it while boxing. In time he took up fencing among other things.

While stationed with the Army in Texas, he met Mamie Dowd, of Boone, Iowa. He proposed to Mamie on Valentine's Day, 1916, and they married on the first of July. Though Ike distinguished himself as a hard worker and organized and effective leader during World War I, he was unable to serve in battle during that war. All of his work was in support and training. It is said that initially during WWII, some of Ike's fellow high-level officers sought to put him down for not having had combat experience during "The Great War." To me, this seems pretty unfair since it is my understanding he actually "wanted" to be involved in combat. I guess life isn't always fair.

During WWII, this Favorite Son of our great state of Kansas proved that sometimes you just can't keep a good guy down. He continued to work hard, and in November 1942 he was made the Supreme Commander of the North African Theater of Operations (NATOUSA). The North Africa campaign was called Operation Torch and was planned underground within the Rock of Gibraltar. In time the results of Operation Torch were good and the Allied Forces prevailed in North Africa. Eisenhower was then involved in the invasions of Sicily and the more challenging invasion of Italy. In December 1943 President Roosevelt chose Ike to be the Supreme Allied Commander in Europe, and he chose him over George Marshall.

Ike proved to be a great leader in many respects. He could even take on dicey, complicated tasks such as when he severely reprimanded General Patton, who at times could be a real turd-bucket. Patton once slapped a subordinate, which you are not supposed to do in the army, and he spoke out of turn on some important foreign policy issues after the war (which were none of his business). Ike managed to scold Patton publicly, but still keep him working since he was effective at many things.

Ike showed an ability to take people on, yet still be able to keep working with them. He had some big-time arguments with Churchill and Field Marshall Montgomery, but still managed to keep good working relationships with them. I would also argue he was insightful to realize that after the war there would be those who would attempt to deny the terrible, awful things that had been done to millions of innocent people by the Nazis (such as the Jewish Holocaust)--that people would try to call these reports propaganda or fake news. Ike ordered extensive documentation of these horrible things with still photographs and movies.

Ike was in charge when the Allied Forces engaged in the D-Day Normandy Landings in June of 1944. This was a terrible but successful invasion. He actually wrote a speech that was to be delivered if the Allied forces lost, which was a distinct possibility. Ike said in this speech that if they lost, and there was any blame or fault--It was his fault.

Wow. What integrity.

After the War, in 1948, Ike was named the President of Columbia University, in New York City, a position he held until January 20, 1953, and I think you can guess why he left this position then. Oh yeah!--A distinguished fellow from Kansas became our President! From my reading, it appears the faculty members at Columbia were not always happy to have him as their president. This is something I do not really understand.

So, in November of 1952, the good people of this great country had the intelligence to elect this Republican from Kansas over a senator from Illinois named Stevenson (which is just fine by me since Danny's last name is Stevenson--the Danny who picked on me last year). And guess what the American people did again four years later in 1956? They again elected Ike over that same Illinois Senator. It makes me almost feel sorry for those people from Illinois and those poor Democrats, but heck, I don't mind saying I'm a Republican, and that we like to win now and then. That is for sure!

Ike fortunately is still around, though Mrs. Snowden said that Ike sightings are now few and far between in his beloved Abilene. He has had some significant health problems over the past decade, but the country still has him and I think he is amazing--an American Hero in my book. I guess he spends most of his time now at a family farm near Gettysburg, Pennsylvania, and at a home in Palm Desert, California. *I am proud to be from Kansas, in part, because I am proud of Ike Eisenhower.*

Wilton Norman Chamberlain is not actually from Kansas, but most of us certainly claim him as one of our own because of his amazing accomplishments while playing basketball for our beloved Kansas University Jayhawks.

Wilt was born one of nine children in Philadelphia, Pennsylvania, to Olivia and William Chamberlain. His mother was a domestic worker and his father a welder and handyman. Wilt was a frail child and almost died of pneumonia. Early on it is said he considered basketball a game for sissies. Instead, he was into track and field activities. My research indicates that in his youth he was able to high jump 6'6", run the 440-yard dash in 49 seconds, and broad jump 22 feet. Eventually he did get involved in basketball, which made sense, because upon entering high school, he was 6'11" tall.

In High School he played for the Overbrook Panthers in Philadelphia. Chamberlain was a standout player in high school. During his senior year he scored 74, 78, and 90 points in a string of three consecutive games. The story is told that while in high school, Red Auerbach, a basketball legend, arranged for Wilt to play a one-on-one game against Kansas University National Champion MVP player of the 1953 season, B.H. Born. Wilt beat Born badly enough in this one-on-one game that he felt very dejected afterward and decided to give up on a promising NBA career. Born instead became a tractor engineer. (Wow, what a poor choice--kind of like me this past winter making weird animal sounds in Mrs.

Snowden's class).

Chamberlain began attending Kansas University in the Fall of 1955. He weighed 240 pounds, was able to reach 9'6" in the air flat footed and was considered a force to be reckoned with. He was put on the KU Freshman team and in his first game the Freshman squad played the Varsity. In the game with the Varsity players he probably hurt a few feelings of some very good players, scoring 42 points, getting 29 rebounds, and achieving four blocked shots. He liked Coach Phog Allen very much, but Coach Allen was forced to retire early on in Wilt's career at Kansas because he turned 70 and the rule was that he had to retire at that age. Wilt did not like the new coach, Dick Harp, nearly as much, which must have been disappointing and frustrating, two emotions I have been familiar with this past year.

His first game for the varsity squad was in December 1956. Wilt scored 52 points in that game and grabbed 31 rebounds, breaking two all-time Kansas records. Chamberlain, in his play, was known for many effective tactics over time, including his finger roll, fade away jump shots, his great passing and of course shot blocking. In the 1956/1957 season our beloved Jayhawks went 13 and 0 until those Oklahoma State Turkey Turds found a legal way to cheat and beat them, making them 13 and 1. Oklahoma State held onto the ball the last 3 ½ minutes of the game with no interest or intent in scoring a basket. They were simply delaying-ball hogs, and it worked, which to me does not seem fair. I hope such tactics don't someday ruin the game of basketball for everyone.

That year, the Jayhawks made it to the NCAA finals and took on the North Carolina Cheating Tarheels. The Tarheels, with Coach Frank McGuire, used some very nasty tactics if you want my opinion. For instance, for the opening tip-off, they put their shortest guy against Wilt--just to mess with his head. Is this really athleticism or sportsmanship? I don't think so. They triple-teamed Wilt most of the evening, and every time he had the ball. Even with all of these very questionable techniques, that had nothing to do with athletic prowess, the game went into overtime at 46 apiece. Somehow those North Carolina Cow Patties managed to eke out a win in the third overtime. Kansans may never forgive them.

His Junior year cannot have been a lot of fun for Wilt. He was so dominating that other teams continued to use these weird strategies against the Jayhawks; freeze-ball approaches, three or more players to guard him, etc., etc. Even still, Chamberlain averaged 30 points a game and the team had an 18-5 record, losing three of those games when he was out sick. Because only the conference winner was invited to the NCAA Tournament, his Junior season was over. When that year ended, he wrote a story: "Why I Am Leaving College Basketball," and sold it to Look magazine for $10,000, and went on to his professional career, which in my opinion is what any sane man would do given such frustrating circumstances. By the way, the average NBA player at that time made $9000 a year.

For the next year (1958/1959) Wilt played for the Harlem Globetrotters. My reading indicates he enjoyed it a lot and they enjoyed him as well. Meadowlark Lemon was the team captain. They made history in 1959 by playing in Moscow. Before the game they were greeted by Nikita Khrushchev, which must have been weird considering that Russia is our enemy.

In the Fall of 1959 Chamberlain started playing for the Philadelphia Warriors, a Philadelphia boy who had come home to make his city proud. He broke eight NBA records his rookie year and was named the NBA MVP. The Warriors made it to the finals that year but the Boston Celtics, coached by Red Auerbach managed to beat them for the championship.

Chamberlain continues to play in the NBA today. He is having an amazing career. On March 2, 1962, in Hershey, Pennsylvania, Wilt scored 100 points in a single game against the New York Knicks.

The Warriors ended up moving to San Francisco but in 1965 Chamberlain was traded to the Philadelphia 76ers and that year the 76ers won it all. Wilt is now a world champion, and who knows what may yet come of his amazing career. Like I said earlier about Ike, *I am proud to be from Kansas, in part, because I am proud of Wilt.* What an amazing basketball career he has had thus far.

As I make a bit of a shift in this rather long letter, let me just say one thing that to the two of you might seem somewhat weird. I just need to say that--***I hate sunglasses.*** I know you must be saying, "What the heck? Why would I be saying this?" But I mean it. ***I hate sunglasses.* I really do.**

So, in our family we are taught to take the Bible pretty seriously, and even though I will admit that I sometimes find Bible reading somewhat boring, I try to read it at least a few times a week for a few minutes. Mom and dad, Pastor Warner, and all of my Sunday school teachers have always said this is a good idea. This past winter, when it came to light that I had misbehaved in Mrs. Snowden's class, dad commented that perhaps I was not spending enough time in Bible reading. I was concerned he was going to institute a rule that there would be a mandatory 30 minutes per day of such reading, and I believe he was tempted, but perhaps he thought the strategy might not work. He commented that perhaps I wasn't reading the Bible enough. There was an awkward silence and so I said he was probably correct. This seemed to calm him down a bit and he said no more.

Recently, I have been reading my Bible more than normal, and I have been looking into some of the passages about which people don't necessarily hear many sermons. Did you guys know that there are a few places where the Bible references giants? I think this is kind of neat. I mean, everyone has heard of the story of David and Goliath, and the bible is pretty clear that Goliath was a giant. I love that story because of the way it ends, though perhaps Goliath was not so fond of the ending. That young, average size David really put it to the big, bad bully who thought he was so very tough. I wish I could have been there to see him take down the big galoot.

But because of the work I did this year on the topic of extraordinary people from Kansas, it got me interested in the idea of extraordinary people referenced in the Bible. The passage that has recently interested me is the first four verses of Genesis 6.

In those verses it says essentially that when men began to multiply on the face of the earth, the sons of God saw that the daughters of men were beautiful, and they took wives for themselves. And, when these wives bore children from these men, these were the mighty men who were of old, men of renown.

In particular, I like the way the King James Version of the Bible states verse 4: "There were giants in the earth in those days; and also after that, when the sons of God came in unto the daughters of men, and they bare children to them, the same became mighty men, which were of old, men of renown."

Now my additional reading tells me that God became quite discouraged about how things were going on earth--he saw that a lot of people had become quite wicked, and this led to him finding Noah, who was still a righteous man. He then told Noah to build an ark, which Noah wisely did, and God decided to do probably the biggest "do-over" of all time. I have already referenced some of my thoughts of the Noah story in an earlier letter to you that you may have read.

What interests me about this passage is that the Bible speaks of giants being on the earth during those days before the great flood. It also speaks of men referred to as "sons of God" taking human wives for themselves and that the children that resulted of these marriages were mighty, which in my book is simply another word for extraordinary.

My reading of the Bible indicates that God wiped out everyone with the great flood, except for Noah and his family. But I have wondered, were there others that did survive, and maybe the writer did not realize it? What about small bands of people that lived in high, mountainous regions? Or was it just Noah and his family that survived? And this passage that says that there were "sons of God" on the earth at one time; it sounds like these were not normal men. The Revised Standard Version of the bible speaks of them as "mighty men" or "men of renown."

I have been asking myself: What were they? Were they angels, or superhumans? Was Noah one of these sons of God, but also right-eous, or was he a normal man? Is it possible that other sons of God later came to the earth and mingled with humans again, after the flood? Perhaps this time these sons of God behaved better, and God saw no reason to wipe them out. I think you can see where this thinking is leading me.

Are there some people among us who aren't completely like the rest of us? How is it that now and then someone is seven feet tall and also athletically graceful, or that another person is simply very great at leading people? How would it be possible that a High School Junior from right here in Wichita, Kansas, could run a mile in under four minutes? How do some people manage to accom-plish the things they do? And Phil Ruger, this guy that lives just five blocks away. How in the heck does he manage to hit the soft-ball farther than anyone else I have ever seen? Is all of this just by chance?

My life, as I think you might appreciate, was turned upside down the day after this past Thanksgiving. I will never think of things the same way again and I am learning to take nothing for granted. I have also learned to keep my mouth shut about certain things I have experienced. It became clear to me after the Thanksgiving event that I needed to view the world with more open eyes. There may be things going on that most people aren't noticing. Frankly, it was also kind of interesting to find something so weird in the Bible. This idea that Giants were once on the earth, and these unique "sons of God" were also here, and they had human wives. That is weird stuff. But, as you know, I am not making it up, and I do indeed wonder--could people like this still be in our world-- among us?

The other thing that has been in my thoughts recently is something you have both probably asked yourselves, though I don't remember ever discussing it with you. We, of course, are a very religious family. And, being so religious, we depend very much on the advice and leadership of ministers. I don't think a day goes by that someone in our family doesn't reference one of the ministers in our lives. Most often Pastor Warner of course, but others as well. Reverend Ogelvy, Reverend Heathcoate, Reverend Thomason or Reverend Kardashian. There are so many, and they have added so much goodness to our lives.

My question is this: What should one do when the minister gets something wrong? I'm not talking about the minister saying something mundane, like, "I doubt it will rain this Sunday. Our plans for the church picnic should turn out fine," and then we have a royal gully-washer. Everyone gets such things wrong from time to time. I'm talking about more substantial mistakes that perhaps in at least small ways change the way we look at things.

Here is an example. There is a minister we all know and love and admire. I won't mention him by name but if I refer to him as Reverend Harbor, I think you will know about whom I am speaking. A week or two ago I was at the Kansas State Camp Meeting at Camp Koinonia listening to him on a rather hot July evening in the open-air tabernacle there. Sometimes for such services I sit near the back and find something fun to do that is quiet enough that I do not get the evil-eye stare from dad, if you know what I mean. But that evening I sat closer to the front just because that is where Clark and Leon went to sit when it was time to get into the services (all the seats near the back were taken by more planful youth and teenagers).

I cannot for the life of me remember exactly what the theme of the sermon was about, but Reverend Harbor had some great stories and of course over time he got wound up a bit and his voice became a bit more enthusiastic and louder and there were quite a number of "Amens" from people in the service. Leon even said Amen once, but I think it was kind of for fun.

At one point, Reverend Harbor was talking about the awesome power of God and the fact that we as people should understand how much less powerful are we, and he went to the current space race between the United States and Russia (the race to get to the moon). I know Reverend Harbor loves the United States, but he said with regard to getting to the moon, that *it will never happen*. I cannot remember his words exactly, but I think they were along the lines of... If God had meant for us to be on the moon, He would have put us there. There were an awful lot of "Amens" to that statement.

The problem is that....I now know that Reverend Harbor got it wrong. One of the movies I have watched on this cellphone I have from the future shows very clearly that in about two years from now, we will get there, and we will beat the Russians (turkeys that they are) and our astronauts will get back safely. Hooray for the USA!!!

By the way, the first line from the astronaut (I think his name is Neil Strongarm) was incredible: "One small step for man, one giant leap for mankind." That was, or in this case will be... amazing! I can't wait to hear it. I think I may throw a party. But I suppose it will have to be planned after the fact since it is probably best I tell no one I know that this is absolutely going to happen.

But, back to the main point. What do we do, or what should we do, when the minister gets something wrong? I mean, they cannot be expected to be perfect. And in the case of Reverend Harbor, how uncomfortable might this be for him in two years? I can just imagine him in the receiving line after a service where he preaches an especially great sermon. Mrs. Joe Schmo might say, "Reverend Harbor, that was a marvelous sermon this morning. It really touched my heart. But I am a little disappointed about your sermon in the summer of 1967 at Camp Koinonia. I wonder, Reverend Harbor, if you have given any thought to that sermon? The one where you declared our great country would never make it to the moon? Well, I guess no one is perfect. But, anyway, it was a wonderful sermon this morning. Thank you."

What is Reverend Harbor supposed to say? "Thank you, Mrs. Schmo, for your wonderful comments about this morning's sermon. And, yes, you are absolutely correct. I was a real schmuck with regard to that sermon in 1967. I only hope the Almighty can see his way to forgive me. I do hope you have a blessed week."

I guess I have to say that I have no answer to this question of what to do when the minister gets it wrong, but it seems like perhaps its a decent question. And guys, I hear dad calling. It sounds like he has something he wants me to do. Perhaps I can continue this letter tomorrow...

PHIL RUGER'S DREAM

Letter Six

Part Two

August 2, 1967

At the end of my writing yesterday, I was asking the question of what to do when the minister gets something wrong. I don't really have an answer, except to say that they cannot be expected to be perfect. I think I have said all that is needed on that topic, so I will continue with my story.

It is Wednesday today and I want to tell you about some things that happened last week. I guess it was Thursday morning. By the way, I am now able to send longer letters to you because I do not have to painstakingly type in every word. When I was typing in Messenger on this thing you call a cellphone, I saw this little picture that looked like a microphone. I pressed it with my finger and said out loud to myself--I have no idea what this does--and it typed for me "I have no idea what this does." It's fair to say that I was pretty shocked to have the phone type for me. I cannot believe such a thing will be possible 50 years from now--it is amazing. Talk about a time saver. But now, how am I going to muster up the energy to practice learning to type, when I know that 50 years from now typing will not be necessary? Why, perhaps I'll just explain to the typing teacher in my upcoming junior high school that this is all a lot of needless work. Perhaps if I tell her I saw something like this on Star Trek or the Jetsons, but then she will just roll her eyes and ask me what kind of grade I want at the end of the year. Sometimes it is really not a lot of fun to know about the future.

Phil normally gives me the cellphone on Wednesday evening at church and I give it back to him on Sunday evening. So, last Wednesday evening, Phil couldn't make it to church. Someone told me he was doing chores for his parents that evening as a punishment because they caught him sneaking out at night, but I am not certain of that story. I didn't ask when he called because it seemed impolite.

But Phil did call me at noon on Wednesday and told me that if I could get over to his house on Thursday at 9:00 in the morning he could give me the phone. He also, somewhat strangely, said he had someone he would like me to meet. I said okay, not having any idea why he might want me to meet someone. In actuality, I didn't feel that I knew Phil that well at that point, let alone him wanting me to meet someone. I was concerned he might want to introduce me to some girl my age that he knows, which is something I could do without. It could be embarrassing. What if the girl is his cousin, and I feel obligated to show all sorts of interest in her? That would not be my idea of a good time.

I normally get up at about 7:00 am, on summer mornings and have breakfast, and do a few chores, like feed the dog or maybe mow the lawn or pull dandelions--no reason to do those things in the hot Kansas summer sun. So, at 8:45, I headed the five blocks to Phil's house. When I turned onto Vine from Munnell Street, I saw a couple of friends, but they looked busy, so I just waved and headed further east toward Phil's place after taking the jog on Vine street to Dayton Avenue. I saw a friend of Sara's riding with someone in a brown 57 Chevy. I could tell it was a 57 because of the big fins on the car. Aren't those 57 Chevys beautiful cars?

I turned left on Phil's street and after passing a couple of houses saw that Phil was sitting alone at the end of his street, under a shade tree, in one of the green lawn chairs that are common in our neighborhood. I don't know what company makes and sells these green lawn chairs--my guess would be Sears and Roebuck, or Montgomery Wards. Those stores sell everything. These green chairs are heavy and kind of ugly, but they are sturdy and last a long time. I swear, you can leave them out through the winter and they still will last several seasons. If you put them in a shed or garage for the winter, they will last almost forever. And they rock, sort of. If you bounce in them, they kind of rock. Phil had two other of the green chairs spaced about five feet from him in triangular fashion as if he was expecting to hold a meeting of sorts. I sat down across from him and was not completely happy to see him, not because I don't like Phil. I do like Phil--but he had sunglasses on--and as I already told you--**I hate sunglasses!** I won't go into why yet, but I do hate them.

The conversation started innocently enough. He asked me how I had been doing and I said fine. He had the cellphone, it appeared, in a paper grocery bag underneath his chair, with a large rubber band around the bag. Then the conversation continued, and it began taking a few turns I wasn't completely expecting.

"I heard you got in a fight, with Danny," said Phil.

I paused for a moment, trying to gather my thoughts, and then uncomfortably said, "That was two months ago. If you were going to bring up that issue with me, I would have expected it before now. How did you learn about it?"

"*I know things,*" responded Phil.

"Okay," I said... Then there was silence, because this was not a topic I liked to discuss. Phil sat in his green chair motionless. I could not read an expression on his face because of the doggone sunglasses.

"So how did it go?"

"How did what go?"

"The fight of course."

"I don't like to talk about it."

This time Phil paused, as if surprised that I wasn't coming across as my normal friendly self.
"Why wouldn't you want to talk about it with me? You came to me for advice about how to handle Danny. I thought you realized I was on your side."

"Oh, sorry. I do appreciate the support you offered. I know you were on my side, and your advice about how to manage a fight was remarkably insightful... I just don't like to talk about it. It was a bad day in my life."

"That is not my understanding."

"Well, I have no idea about your understanding."

"I understand you won."

"Won what."

"The fight."

"Oh, that." "I don't know the source of your information but I suppose some would say I won."

"Well did you?"

"It depends on how you define winning, I guess."

"What the heck are you talking about?"

"Does a person win if he shames himself?"

"I don't know what you mean."

"I have been taught at church that fighting is not the way to go. Someone once asked Jesus if it is enough to forgive someone seven times if they offend you. I think you know the rest of the story. Jesus said the answer is seven times seventy. On the night of the crucifixion, when the unruly crowd came to get Jesus, to kill him, Peter started a serious fight with a fellow, almost killing him. Jesus turned to Peter and told him no way. This is not the way we do things. Jesus was clearly against such responses."

"So you think you were wrong to fight?"

"My Sunday school teacher told me that fighting is not what we stand for."

"But I heard Danny picked on you, again and again, and for a very long time."

"That part is true."

"If you weren't wanting to fight, what put you over the edge? He must of done something to really get your goat."

"You are right about that too. He started making fun of me that I liked a girl in the class."

"Did you?"

"Did I what?"

"Did you like the girl?"

"Yeah. But that was none of his business."

"I completely agree. He had no business continuing to mess with you in such ways."

"So," continued Phil, "Danny is like five inches taller than you and you still decided to fight him?"

"I was really mad. He could have been Wilt Chamberlain, and I would have fought him. It didn't matter."

"You know, the third chapter of Ecclesiastes says, 'There is a time for all things.' Perhaps there is even a time for fighting. I think you were very much within your rights to take action to put a stop to his monkey business."

"I've never heard you quote scripture before."

Phil paused. "You think just because I am our church's bad boy, I can't quote scripture now and then?"

"I didn't mean it that way, Phil. I don't think of you that way."

"I'm not offended. I don't quote scripture very often. You're right about that."

Phil continued, "I understand Danny was the guy who ended up on the ground at the end of the fight. Is that true?"

"You know, I haven't talked about this with anyone other than my parents and the principal, and my buddies, Robert and Ronnie, and my Quaker friend who was there as a witness to the fight. How do you know these things?"

"I already told you. *I know things*."

"What is that supposed to mean?"

"It just means *I know things*. So was he the one who ended up on the ground?"

"I really don't like to talk about this, Phil. I did not behave the way I have been taught in church that I should behave. It is very unpleasant to discuss."

"I see, " said Phil, and he said nothing more. There was again this awkward silence. And, I could not tell what was going on with Phil, because I could not see his eyes. Those darn sunglasses. I felt I was being interrogated, perhaps even messed with, by a guy who had never in the past been anything but kind to me. I mean, let me be clear. I am aware Phil has a tough side. As stories go in the neighborhood, a number of fellows bigger than him have learned the hard way it is best to not try to mess with Phil--if you do so, it is at your own peril. But he had always been good to me. I could not figure out what was going on. Couldn't he tell that for me this was an embarrassing and uncomfortable topic? Why did he persist? But the conversation only got more complicated from there. Phil changed the topic. "How is your family?"

"They are good. I think everyone is doing well. Sara got married this summer. The wedding went well."

"Do you like the fellow she married?"

"Yeah. He is a real good guy. He has a great motorcycle."

"Are your parents doing well?"

"Sure. My dad has some back problems, but otherwise they are doing well."

"Are your sisters both okay?"

"Yeah. Sara seems happily married from what I can tell. Kara seems like she may turn out to be a musical virtuoso. She is very young but can play the piano like nobody's business, without lessons, and can she ever sing. By the time she is 12, she may end up on Lawrence Welk."

"How about your brothers? How are they doing?"

"They are doing well. Ray is a guy who can fix things. Almost anything. I am not like that at all. I'm better at breaking things if truth be told. JW is only 6, so its still hard to tell what he will become. He is just so nice. Little kids love him. Older kids think he is funny. He gets along well with everyone."

Phil paused again, then he asked, "How about your other brothers?"

I was taken completely off guard by this unexpected question. This very personal part of my life had never been discussed with Phil. I felt like someone had just hit me in the gut, and hard. It took my breath away. I paused, gathered my thoughts, realized that I could not see through those darn sunglasses to read his eyes, and said firmly, "Perhaps you took a crazy pill this morning, Phil. I don't know what you're talking about. I have two brothers and that is all."

It seems Phil was able immediately to read the emotion in my voice. "Well, well," he said, "I didn't mean to get you angry. I hope you don't take after me like you did poor Danny. I might just end up the loser, I suppose. Perhaps I too, will have a couple of broken ribs."

"Very funny, Phil, my older friend who happens to be twice my size, and who is a football star for the West High Pioneers." I paused, again reeling internally from the shift in his questioning. "I didn't mean to respond with anger. I simply do not know at all what you are talking about. I have two brothers and that is it."

"I am not sure you are telling me the whole truth," replied Phil, and then he paused.

"Aren't you taught in church to always tell the truth?"

Then it became my turn to pause, but just briefly, and I remembered the words of a famous coach--the best defense is often a good offense. "Why are you messing with me, Phil?" This time I allowed my anger to be a bit more evident. "You have never been anything other than nice and decent to me. Do you feel like picking on a younger kid, today? Does it make you feel more powerful? I understand you are pretty popular with the teenage girls. Perhaps we should get one of your teenage girl fans over here so that you can beat up on me and look like the king of the neighborhood. The only problem is that I hate to have to start thinking of you as a doggone bully."

This time Phil was the one who seemed taken aback. He was surprised at my intensity. "Now calm down, Carson. Don't jump so quickly to the conclusion that I'm mistreating you. You know I don't do that to you. I mess with Jay Bowser now and then, just to keep him in line, but I still like him, and besides, he is pretty much my size. I just happen to think you do have other brothers, and I want to know more about them."

I was feeling very much beside myself with this unexpected line of inquiry. I paused, and then it came to me. "I get it, Phil. Why didn't I think of this earlier? Your mom is a great lady. Of course, this is it. My mom probably went to Ruger's Laundry Mat this past winter to do some laundry. She was worried about me and some of the crazy things I had been saying and she confided in your mom. I just don't know why your mom would have shared this with you. My mom would have shared such things in confidence, and your mom is a terrific lady."

"No, you have it all wrong, Carson. I did not hear these things from my mom, though I do appreciate your kind words about her. I could say the same types of things about your mother. She is a mother to all. You aren't listening carefully to me this morning.

As I have already said several times--*I know things.*"

"What the heck does that mean, Phil? And if you know so much, why don't you tell me about these older brothers you believe I have and that you seem to know so much about?" I was still irritated and decided that if he was going to be such a wise guy, I might as well give him some of his own medicine. I was shocked that Phil would treat me this way and then pretend to still be a nice guy.

There was a period of silence again, and once again there were those darn sunglasses, so I could see absolutely no expression on his face. Finally he said, "I have already told you I know they were older, I also happen to know they were twins, identical to be more specific, and they were very nice fellows."

The emotion grew within me as I continued to feel irritated and I was ready to let him know it. I had no doubt the terrible outcome if I were to fight Phil Ruger, but I had just about had enough of this two-bit son of a gun messing with me. I was starting to feel the way I felt before I decided to fight Danny. I no longer cared what might happen. The difference is I stood zero chance of winning this fight.

"So, Mister Smart-ass."

"Wait a second, Carson, you are so involved at the church. You don't talk like this. Christians don't talk like this."

"I occasionally do these days when I have had it up to here with someone. Some of the things I have been through this year have changed me. I believe difficult events in life sometimes change people... "If you know so many things, as you claim, why don't you please tell me their names."

"I don't know their names."

"Just as I thought." You are messing with me. You're a turkey turd, just like Danny. I would have never guessed... And I thought you were a good guy, like Jay Bowser. You are nothing like him. When I treated Jay badly, he realized I was having a hard time and even though he didn't understand what I was going through, he forgave me." And with that, I stood up abruptly to walk away, without the beloved cellphone.

I was three steps away from Phil when I heard him say, "But I know what they look like."

I spun around, still angry, and said "Oh yeah, well please enlighten me, Mr. Fellow who says he 'knows things,' because I don't think you know shit, quite honestly."

"I hate to hear you talking like this. Members of your family don't talk this way. Maybe something has indeed happened in your life that has changed you." He paused as if searching within his memory banks. "Your brothers look exactly alike, and they have red hair."

I didn't even pause with this one. "Great guess, Dr. Einstein, everyone knows three of my four siblings have red hair. You know nothing." I glared at him, not caring what happened to me and whether I ever talked with this butthead again. How could I have missed the fact that he is just another schmuck?

He paused for another moment, then he said, "Their hair wasn't exactly red. No...more specifically, it was auburn, and until this summer they played softball with me on the church team, and they were very good. Really nice guys. One was a pitcher and one was a catcher. You came with them to every one of their games.

You were their biggest fan. This is why you came to all of our games this year, even though you are not yet old enough to play. This is why you came to most of our practices."

My internal rage went immediately to numbness and I'm certain all color left my face. I went to the other side of the shade tree and vomited.

Then I returned to my green chair and sat in it once again. After finally regaining my composure I asked, "How do you know these things, Phil? No one could guess these things, and no one besides me knows these things. Not even my parents nor my brothers and sisters. I asked my mom and dad so many times last November and December why there were three beds in the basement where I sleep when there is only one of me. They could not answer.

"No one, including my mom, has told me anything," said Phil.

"On Monday night I had a dream and they were in it and somehow I knew them, and I liked them, and I saw that you were with them and it was clear they were your brothers." When I awakened it started to make sense to me why you have taken such an interest in the church softball team this summer.

I was starting to feel tired, as if worn out by the unexpected emotions. "You dreamed this?"

"Yes, and I need you to promise me that you will never tell anyone about my dream."

"Why? At long last I have finally found someone who knows for sure what I have been through this past year and that I am not crazy. Why would you ask me to endure further pain by telling no one?"

"I can't explain it right now but let me be clear that if you care about me at all, it is essential that you tell no one about my dream, not ever."

Then Phil said, "So I have to assume that this device I came up with that appears to be from the future, must have something to do with this matter of your brothers who have gone missing. Am I right about this?"

I nodded. (Sorry, guys, it is dinner time and Church is this evening--Wednesday evening. It's a good thing Phil let me borrow the phone for some extra days this week. I'll try to write more tomorrow).

UNCLE DAVE

Letter 6

Part Three

August 3, 1967

...continued...

"**I** can't explain it right now, but let me be clear that if you care about me at all, it is essential that you tell no one about my dream, not ever," said Phil.

"You mean the dream you had about my brothers?" I asked.

"Yes," said Phil.

"It seems kind of crazy," I suggested. "But if it's that important to you, I promise."

"It is," said Phil.

Then Phil said, "So I have to assume that this device I came up with that appears to be from the future, must have something to do with this thing of your brothers who have gone missing. Am I right about this?"

I nodded.

"I would bet you have seen your brothers in the future on the movies, haven't you?"

Again, I nodded.

"I thought the movies were all fantasy, so I've paid them little attention. Have you seen your parents?"

"No, but I have done the math. In 2016, dad would be 95 and mom would be 89. I suppose they cannot live forever though that is hard to think about. There have been many things this past eight months that I have thought about that I would have preferred never to consider.

"Have you seen yourself?"

"No. Only them."

"How can you be so sure it is them. The color of their hair would not still be auburn."

"That is just it. I can't be sure it is them. The movies may indeed be all fantasy. In many ways I hope they are, because some of the things that appear to be going on fifty years from now cause me to worry. Yet, this is my only connection with my brothers who went missing, so there is of course a big part of me that wants the movies to be real. It gives me some hope that in the future I might again find them."

Phil and I spent some time talking about some of the things I had seen in the movies on the phone. Movies of things that are apparently going on fifty years in the future. I explained that as time had progressed there were more movies, as if I was receiving weekly or monthly updates. I explained what some of my primary worries were and some of the things that had apparently developed in the future that cause me such confusion.

"So," said Phil, "We really do get to the moon. That is incredible. Do the K.U. Jayhawks win any National Football Championships?"

"That has been one of my main questions too, and unfortunately I have no answer. There has been so little information on these movies about sports. In one of the few brief movies I saw about sports, the announcer started talking about King James--which I thought was really weird. Why would he start talking about the Bible in the middle of a sports story?"

Phil shrugged. "That makes no sense to me either. Sounds crazy."

After I shared with him some of the main things about the future that had me worried, we sat silently for a minute or two. Then Phil broke the silence as if he was a man on a mission, and said, "Like I said on the phone yesterday, I want you to meet someone."

"You want me to meet someone? Okay. I guess with what I have been through thus far this morning, I might as well meet someone. Who is it--The Abominable Snowman perhaps?"

"No, just my uncle who is visiting," and Phil yelled toward the house, "Uncle Dave, can you come out here for a few minutes? Uncle Dave?"

From within his house, I heard someone say, "Okay, Phil, I'll be there in a moment."

Next, an elderly gentleman sauntered from Phil's house about a minute later, dressed all in khaki, khaki slacks, a khaki shirt, and a broad brimmed khaki hat, and you surely know what else he was wearing. That's right, he wore over-sized, dark sunglasses. Why did he have to wear sunglasses? **I hate sunglasses!**

He sure looked like an Uncle to Phil. About the same height, just under six feet, I suppose, though with a bit of a stoop. You could tell that in an earlier day he had Phil's broad shoulders and athletic build. It appeared to me his health was not great, though, at this stage. He walked slowly, though even so, still conveying a certain confidence about himself in spite of his noticeably weakened posture produced presumably by the passage of time.

Phil's uncle took a seat in the third green chair that was available, but before he did Phil introduced us.

"Uncle Dave, this is Carson, a young friend of mine. This is the young fellow I was talking to you about yesterday when you arrived and you said you would like to meet and speak with him." Phil then turned to me and said, "You may have heard at church that I was being punished yesterday for misbehavior, which was why I missed church. I was actually at home last evening talking with Uncle Dave."

Before taking a seat, Uncle Dave held out his hand to shake mine. He grabbed it firmly and said, "Its nice to meet you young man. Phil has told me some very nice things about you. He also told me you come from a very good and decent family."

"Thank you, sir. I do come from a good family. It is nice of you to say this. Phil comes from a very fine family as well. His father and mother and older brother are all great people. I did not know he had an uncle. It is a pleasure to meet you, sir." (I was hoping this conversation was almost over. I did not know what else to say. I had said everything polite that I could think of, but I was also a bit unprepared for the reality that Phil's uncle was more of a conversationalist than one might have expected).

Uncle Dave took a seat in the sturdy green chair and started the conversation directly and quite unexpectedly, "Let me come right to the point, young man. I have a few questions for you. I would like to know about your brothers."

I started feeling weird again, a bit dizzy, and a little sick to my stomach, not expecting a direct question of this sort from someone I did not know. I did manage the presence of mind to say, "I was just discussing this very issue with Phil, sir. I have two younger brothers. One is a fellow who seems able to fix about anything. Unfortunately, I am not like that. My youngest brother is just so very likeable. I want to become more like both of them, if I am able."

"No, no, young man, you are missing my point. I want to know about your older brothers, the brothers Phil told me about who went missing." His statement was followed simply by silence.

This time I did not feel hit in the gut. I felt kicked, as if by a mule. What was going on in my world? Why was I again suddenly feeling under attack? What would come next? Was Phil out to get me after all?

"Sir, I don't know exactly what Phil has told you. Phil had a dream that I have two older brothers. His dream was very specific. This has been a very unusual year in my life, sir, but this is clearly not something I feel comfortable talking about with someone I have just met. I mean no disrespect."

I was kind of thinking that by letting Phil's Uncle Dave know that he was making me uncomfortable, he would back down a bit, but I quickly learned that Uncle Dave was not a man of that demeanor. Instead, he continued, "Of course you mean no disrespect, and none is taken young man. However, my driver will be here in just a few minutes and I really have several questions that I need answered. And, further, I am going to need to ask that the conversation I have with you be kept confidential though I cannot necessarily promise that what you tell me will be treated in the same fashion."

My head was still spinning as I was trying to process what this very intense, and clearly intelligent uncle to Phil was saying when he made his next unexpected move...

He took off his sunglasses...I was stunned. No, I was more than stunned...I simply do not have an appropriate word to express how I felt when Uncle Dave took off his glasses. The face was absolutely unmistakable. Phil's Uncle Dave was none other than Dwight David Eisenhower.

"Do you know who I am, young man?" he asked, as he promptly returned his sunglasses to his face.

"Yes, sir. You are one of the most revered men in the world to both of my parents. My father is a veteran, sir, and I have no doubt he would gladly take a bullet for you. My mother speaks of you with such admiration."

"Well, your parents sound like very good and decent people and I am honored by the esteem in which they hold me. If indeed I am held in such esteem by your parents, is it not then reasonable, as difficult as it might be, that I ask that you to please never tell your parents, nor any family member, nor any of your friends, other than Phil, that you have met me or spoken with me. Do I have your assurance on this matter?"

"Yes, sir," was all that I could offer.
"Phil tells me that you are a young man who can be trusted to keep his word. Is this true?"

"Yes sir. But if I attempt to send messages to my brothers in the future about this meeting, would that be okay?"

"Well, its hard for me to imagine how that could hurt anything. If Phil tells you it is okay, its okay. The main person I am trying to protect with this secrecy is Phil."

"Why would that be, sir? How could your secrecy protect Phil?"

"That is a reasonable and perceptive question, young man, and it is deserving of an answer. The reason I am visiting your friend, Phil, is the same reason that I have visited him numerous times over the past decade or so, though this is only the second time I have been to his home, as a matter of maintaining his anonymity. I visit Phil because it just so happens that *Phil knows things*.

"I kind of thought you were going to say that, sir."

"I see. Well it does happen to be the case that somehow or another, Phil indeed does at times seem to know things, and sometimes the things he knows are helpful for people in high places to know, and so I try to pass along information to those in power if it seems it might be useful.

But it would be very risky for me to be seen with Phil. If some of our high-level security experts were to find out about him, and his abilities, he would never be allowed to live a normal life, or to live the life that he might want to choose for himself. So, normally his parents take him to out of the way places near Abilene for me to talk with him. And, of course, much of our conversations occur by phone, especially since my health has been fading. I had to pull some strings several years ago to get Bell Telephone to install as special phone line to his home so that his family was no longer on a party line. That took a bit of finagling."

"Phil's parents became aware of his ability to 'know' certain things when he was only three or four, according to his mother. She tells me the first incident was May 25, 1955. Phil had been put to bed at 8:00 pm, and awoke an hour later screaming inconsolably and weeping. He just kept saying, 'The storm... the winds... get away.' His mom tried to comfort him letting him know that there had been some nearby storms but all was well. 95 minutes later a tornado wiped the town of Udall, Kansas, off the map, killing 80 people and injuring 200 more. I was president, of course, at the time. A newsman I spoke with the next week, who had visited Udall, said the site was unlike anything he had ever seen. Phil's mother initially did not know what to think. But as time passed, and Phil reliably forecasted more and more events, she knew something unusual was going on. In my view, she exercised very good judgment by keeping the secret within the family--just his mother and father and brother know of Phil's ability to 'know things.' In time they were able to connect with me."

"Phil was able to convey some information and ideas to me while I was still in office, and he was not yet even ten years of age, that proved pretty helpful in terms of how I was thinking of a couple of complicated matters. But it was during the Cuban Missile Crisis that he proved extraordinarily helpful. He had a dream that provided insight that might never have been considered. I think he was only 11 or 12 at the time. His mom gave him permission to call me about the dream he had and it caused me to think of the situation in such a different way. I called Jack that very day and shared this new way of thinking of the situation."

"Jack, sir?" I asked.

"Oh, sorry. Jack Kennedy is who I called. We were of different political parties and we had our differences, but we both loved this country."

"Oh, I see," was all I could say.

Uncle Dave continued, "I still regret so much that the phone line was down at the Pennsylvania farm on November 21, 1963. Phil tried several times to call me to tell me that he had a dream about a shooting at a book store in Dallas. There was a shooting alright, that came from a book depository the very next day and I am convinced that terrible day may forever effect the very psyche of our wonderful country. If only the phone line had been working. But this is how life sometimes occurs. Some things do seem to occur by chance. It is so important to be thoughtful and especially planful, but life has away of happening that can foil many of our very best plans." Uncle Dave seemed lost in thought for a moment.

Phil interrupted, "Uncle Dave, I am aware your driver may be coming soon. Let me mention that Carson has watched these movies on this device that appears to be from 50 years in the future. He says that most of the movies are news reports, and that strangely enough there are other movies that appear to be of conversations people are having in church basements or church fellowship halls. Carson says that if these movies are really from the future there are some things that will be going on 50 years in the future that have him pretty worried. I did not know this earlier in the week when I called you."

"Well, what makes you think, young man, that these movies and news reports, from 50 years in the future, might be the real deal?"

"Because I think I have seen my missing brothers, though admittedly I cannot be sure."

"And what is your theory about how your brothers went missing?"

"Have you ever watched Star Trek, sir? And are you familiar with Einstein's theory of the space-time continuum?"

"Well I have managed in the past year to watch one Star Trek episode. I am familiar with Einstein, as I have met him on a couple of occasions. He came across as a bit of an odd duck to me, but I suppose with such genius can come a bit of oddity."

"Well, sir, I believe that either I, or my brothers, may have been caught up in what could be called a time warp, at least that is what Spock called such a thing in Star Trek, and the idea seems to fit with Einstein's suggestion that time can be flexible rather than rigid as we tend to assume. This leaves my brothers and me in parallel universes."

"I see. What are some of these things that may occur 50 years in the future that cause you such concern?"

"I guess my biggest concern is that if these movies are real, we will elect a president 50 years in the future who is what I would call a super bully, and who doesn't like people of other races, and who lies a lot."

"Now, that does not sound encouraging. I hope the last name is not Patton or McCarthy--talk about pains in the proverbial rump of this country."

"No sir, his last name is not either of those. His first name is Donald."

"Can you provide me with any examples of his behavior?"

"Sure. From the movies I have watched, I have honestly never seen or even heard of the kind of bullying he displayed. He would definitely have been expelled by the principal at my elementary school for his bullying behaviors. A lot of his most fierce bullying behaviors were done during his presidential campaign. He is a Republican like me and my parents, and like you and Mrs. Eisenhower."

"Well, I can imagine he might have done a bit of bullying of his Democratic opponent, young man; the Democrats can at times be harsh themselves."

"No, sir, I am mainly talking about the way he treated the other Republican candidates who were running against him in the presidential primary."

"You must be kidding me."

"No, sir. One of his main opponents was a man named Jeb. Jeb's father and brother had already served as presidents. This fellow made fun of Jeb without mercy, mainly calling him 'Low-energy Jeb.' It was remarkable. In time, Jeb dropped out of the race though he had been leading. And, there was a senator from Texas that at first, he was friends with, at least it seemed. His name was Ted. In time Donald started calling him 'Lying Ted.' He called him Lying Ted so many times that it stuck, though it was not at all clear that Ted was a liar. Ted dropped out of the race. There was a senator from Florida whose name was Marco and this one was really irritating to me. Marco was quite a bit shorter than Donald and so Donald started calling him 'Little Marco.' He called him Little Marco so many times that it again seemed to kind of stick. Marco didn't seem to know quite what to say--he dropped out too. I couldn't believe it."

When I watched the movies of the election process it all seemed so wild. Plus, Donald seemed to be a close buddy to the President of Russia, which made no sense to me, because Russia seems to not be our friend, and many people in the news reports also expressed worry about Donald being such a close buddy to the Russian President, so I got the idea Russia is still not our friend 50 years in the future.

"Don't you mean Soviet Union, young man? asked Uncle Dave.

"A good point, sir. No. They are no longer calling it the Soviet Union. They are calling it Russia."

"That is interesting," said Uncle Dave.

"So, this fellow, Donald, was elected president of our great country?"

"He was sir, and quite a number of experts at the time expressed the idea that the Russians in some way interfered with the U.S. election to help Donald get elected."

"Extraordinary," said Uncle Dave. "Those Russians should not be trusted... They are not our friends."

"When it comes to the lying, it was the Democrat, a lady, who got 3 million more votes than Donald, but Donald won in the Electoral College, and after the election he claimed that the votes had been wrong, and that he not only won in the Electoral College but also in the popular vote. And he said that the talk of Russian interference in the election, which was agreed upon by our intelligence experts, was all nonsense. Then, early in his presidency, whenever a journalist would say something he didn't like, even though the journalist might have been respected by many for years, he would refer to the journalist and accuse him or her of spreading fake news."

"Oh, my goodness," said Uncle Dave. "Let's hope all of these movies are nothing more than fantasy. This sound both frightening and unbelievable."

"I could not agree more, sir."

"Your reports create concern for me, young man, though I am not sure there is anything that can be done at this point, in 1967. Is there anything else that you have seen and heard that concerns you?"

"Yes, sir. There is one more area of concern."

"And what is that."

"I am concerned, sir, about my people."

"What do you mean by – 'your people.'"

"Evangelicals, sir. I come from a very religious family, and we are Evangelicals."

"You mean Christians?"

"Yes, sir, although I think there are some Christians that might not be considered Evangelicals."

"What concerns you about your people – about Evangelicals"

"Most of them supported Donald, who was elected President, and when he continued lying about important matters after the election, they did not demand his behaviors change. They continued to accept whatever he said or did even when it was clearly wrong, and even when his behavior was sinful. It makes no sense to me."

"Blessed Mother Mary," Ike said softly.

"What, sir?"

"Oh, nothing."

"Are there other concerns?"

"Well, a lot of Evangelicals appear to be carrying guns wherever they go."

"Now this does sound like fantasy, young man. Christians are a peaceful people. Why in heaven's name would they be carrying guns?"

"I've had the same reaction myself, Uncle Dave. It makes no sense to me. My father never carries a gun, except when he goes quail hunting, but lots of Evangelicals are definitely carrying guns."

"And who, pray tell, is encouraging this?"

"The National Rifle Association, it appears."

"The National Rifle Association? Ike responded.

"Yes sir."

"You must be kidding me," Ike continued. "They are very much about gun safety. If I remember right, their original purpose or motto had to do with gun safety, marksmanship, and I suppose shooting for sport. Why would they be encouraging people to carry guns with them in their daily lives? That doesn't sound safe at all. More than that, what is the result of so many people carry-ing guns?"

"The country is experiencing lots and lots of mass shootings, in part because guns have become so much more effective and they are mass produced, like Henry Ford did with cars. Lots of people have many, many guns. Many people have guns that can fire hun-dreds of rounds in a small amount of time. It only takes a few nuts to do a lot of damage."

"Mary, Joseph, and Methuselah."

"What, sir?"

"Oh, it's just an expression I picked up during the war."

"So," Mr. President,

"Please call me Uncle Dave, like your friend, Phil. It is so important I not be identified when with Phil."

"Oh, yes, sure. So, Uncle Dave, is there some method you have for getting messages through to the future? It seems it would be very helpful to our country if this is possible."

"Unfortunately, young man, I know of no such possibility. Your friend, Phil, is the closest thing I have ever seen. He has these unusual dreams that appear to forecast the future, and even those can be very difficult to interpret, and they only forecast a few days into the future."

"Okay, but you said that you have met Dr. Einstein. Is he still alive and would you be able to speak with him about these matters? About whether it is possible to get messages to the future."

"Unfortunately, he died a little more than a decade ago. I suppose I might be able to inquire about some of his associates and students but getting help from such sources would seem like a long shot."

"But what about Phil's other connections to the future?" Out of the corner of my eye, I saw Phil shift uncomfortably in his chair when I asked this question.

"I guess I do not know of what you speak when you mention his other connections."

"Phil came up with this device that appears to be from 50 years in the future. I have been concluding that Phil must somehow have contacts with people who do time traveling, or that perhaps Phil is a time traveler. I just assumed you would know about such possibilities."

Uncle Dave paused and turned his attention to Phil, and hesitated, but then asked. "Is there something you would like to tell me Phil about how you came about acquiring this device from what appears to be out of the future?"

Phil paused for most of a minute, his face unreadable because of the sunglasses. Finally, he said, "Uncle Dave, I think there are some stories of my life and experiences thus far that perhaps should be left untold."

Uncle Dave now paused briefly, and then said, "I've heard similar statements before, mainly from our spies in Europe during the Second War. At first, such statements bothered me, but in time I learned to take them seriously. If you believe there are some things you should not tell me, I will accept your conclusion. I feel certain you have your reasons."

Ike paused for a moment, then looked up and saw his car coming. He stood up and said, "I apologize, but I am sure Mamie is waiting for me. It has been a pleasure to meet you, young man. I hope somehow you find your brothers. I also hope all you have told me about the future proves to be fantasy."

"I agree with you, sir, completely. And let me say that what started out as an emotional and challenging day in my life has led to...um...quite an honor, sir--meeting you."

"You are very gracious. I am sorry that we may not meet again. And Phil, I won't be able to drop by your house in the future. It appears Mamie and I will be mainly living in California soon, rather than back and forth between Pennsylvania and California. I will try to make sure my phone number stays the same, but should it change I will get it to you. And to you, young man, Phil has a special address to which he can send me personal letters. You can send letters to that post office box as well. Those letters will be opened by me and me alone."

"Thank you, sir."

Uncle Dave stood, straightening himself, and then turned to me one last time and said, "By the way, young man, have my beloved K.U. Jayhawks won any national football titles in the next 50 years?"

"Phil was asking me the same thing just an hour or so ago, sir. I have received so little sports information in these movies. I simply do not know. I apologize."

"Oh, that's okay. I just would like to see them win one," as he turned toward the arriving car.

"Thanks for visiting, Uncle Dave," said Phil.

"It was my pleasure, Phil. Thank you for your assistance over the years."

And with that, Ike got into the back seat of a dark sedan with tinted windows and he left.

After Uncle Dave left, Phil and I did some talking. He asked me additional questions about the two of you. He wanted to know more about how involved you had been on the softball team, whether he had been friends with you guys, who your girlfriends had been, and all sorts of questions. I told him honestly that you had both liked him quite a lot, though you were not his closest friends, and that you were also good buddies with his older brother, Rob. Phil seemed to have kind of a weird reaction in this discussion, almost as if he was feeling like he had just lost two friends, though he obviously possessed no specific memories of you. He only had the images that came to him in his dream, and the things I had shared with him about you guys.

He commented that losing the two of you in such an odd and unexpected fashion must have been really tough on me. It felt really good to finally have another person in my world who seemed to understand this unusual trauma in my life. He asked me how I was able to keep going. I told him there are still so many good things in my life, and that I have hope of finding you guys in the future, and that I know that the two of you would want me to be okay.

He must have been feeling protective of me somewhat because he even asked me if I needed him to go have a one-on-one talk with Danny, just to make sure that in the future Danny would not be tempted to think it might be a good idea to cause me additional trouble. I told Phil that I still do not feel ready to discuss what happened with Danny, and how I handled it, but that with what did transpire, I did not think additional assistance was needed.

Phil then walked me over to Bowser's Burger Bar, bought me a hamburger from the grill and two bottles of coke. That made for a great ending to a really emotional morning.

At Bowser's Burger Bar, they had an outdoor table where we could talk and I explained to Phil that 50 years in the future our country apparently has a completely new kind of mail; that they call it Email and that I can only assume E stands for excellent. I mentioned that there appear to be different types of Email, and that one of them is Gmail, and that I am thinking G probably stand for great. I explained that instead of people having one address for a family, it appears everyone has their own address. He asked me where in the world they would put so many mail boxes, and I told him that was exactly my question. I mentioned that it appears people in the future get to name their own specific mailboxes and we had a lot of fun thinking about what we might want to name our mailboxes if he and I were able to have our own. I told him mine would maybe be CarsonDodge67@gmail.com. He said he had heard some really neat stories from Uncle Dave about the

Smokey Hill River and so he thinks he would want his to be Phil-Rugerofthesmokeyhillriver@gmail.com. We had a lot of fun with that discussion.

So, that's what is going on here. It's almost lunchtime. Uncle Ray and Aunt Wynona are supposed to visit this afternoon. Dad said he and Uncle Ray may take me fishing at Camp Koinonia. That should be fun. I hope the catfish are biting. I hope you guys are doing well 50 years in the future.

Your brother,

Carson

Made in the USA
Middletown, DE
21 September 2020

20248585R00059